THE AMARNA PRINCESSES : BOOK 2

CATALYST

KYLIE QUILLINAN

First published in Australia in 2022.

ABN 34 112 708 734

kyliequillinan.com

A catalogue record for this book is available from the National Library of Australia

Ebook ISBN: 9781922852045

Paperback ISBN: 9781922852090

Large print ISBN: 9781922852106

Hardcover ISBN: 9781922852113

Cover art by Deranged Doctor Design.

Edited by MS Novak.

LP09092023

ONE
TEY

"Neb," I called. "Sensen. Come eat while it is hot."

The two girls who came running over looked nothing like the princesses I fled Akhetaten with two years ago. They were taller and their dark skin was now sun-browned. Nef was ten years old, long-legged and possessing her mother's effortless elegance. Seti was nine, a little chubbier than her sister, and wild.

They flung themselves down on the blanket where Hennie and I sat, and reached for the food. Around us, other children returned to their families as the Sand Wanderers settled in for the evening meal. Children often went to whichever group they chose, and it was a rare night when Hennie and I ate with both girls and none of their friends.

A large central campfire gave us plenty of light to see by as the sun sank below the horizon, far away across an endless desert. Small groups sat at different points around the fire. The tribe mostly comprised the families of the sons of Old Man, the Sand Wanderers' chief. We were the only tribe members not related by blood or marriage.

I studied Nef and Seti as they gulped down the soft white cheese we ate with bread and olive oil. Where Nef's hair hung to her shoulders in neat braids, Seti's was a tangled knot that looked like it hadn't met a comb in months. Nef kept her clothes tidy and almost always wore sandals, whereas every day Seti seemed to have a new hole in her sleeve or a frayed hem on her skirt. Her feet were typically bare and dirty.

"What did you do today?" I asked.

Seti didn't reply, too intent on eating as fast as possible. Nef, always the politer of the two, set down her bread while she answered.

"We built a sand fort and hid inside it," she said. "We pretended we had run away and men were searching for us."

It was interesting how often their games revolved around fleeing and hiding. Seti swallowed the last of her food and licked her fingers.

"I am finished," she said. "May I go?"

"Come give your grandmother a hug first, Sensen," Hennie said. Despite how long we had lived with the Sand Wanderers, we still always used our cover names. It had been a long time since Seti had complained about being called Sensen. "I have hardly seen you for days."

Seti cast a glance back towards her friends, but seeing the other girls were still eating, she allowed Hennie to pull her in for a hug.

"Oh, phew." Hennie pushed her away. "Sensen, you reek. When did you last bathe?"

"I don't know."

"Have you bathed at all since we arrived here?" Hennie asked.

"Maybe?"

The look on Seti's face indicated she was sure she hadn't bathed since the last oasis.

"First thing tomorrow morning," I said. "I don't want to see you at breakfast until you have bathed."

"Yes, Mama."

Seti's immediate acquiescence meant she had little intention of complying. I told myself to remember to make sure she did bathe tomorrow. Mothering the girls didn't come easily to me and I often forgot to remind them about things like bathing or wearing a clean tunic. I figured they would do it themselves when they smelled bad enough, but perhaps I needed to pay more attention. It seemed smelling vile was no deterrent for Seti.

"I mean it, Sensen," I said. "There will be no breakfast for you if you come without having bathed."

"Uh huh. Can I go now?"

Nef set down her bowl. "I am finished too and I bathed yesterday. May I leave?"

"I am sure your grandmother will want a hug from you too, especially if you smell better than Sensen," I said. "You can both go, but Neb, please remind your sister when she wakes up tomorrow that she needs to bathe."

Nef hugged Hennie, and the girls ran off.

"I suppose they have more important things to think about than cleanliness," Hennie said.

We were silent for a few moments, watching as the girls quickly became immersed in a new game with their friends, until I realised I hadn't replied.

"It does not excuse Sensen from not bathing until she smells worse than a donkey," I said. "But I don't think they have ever had friends before. I suppose this is all still new and exciting for them."

The girls had adapted to life with the Sand Wanderers with apparent ease, swiftly making friends with the other girls, although I had forbidden them from revealing their identities or their real names to any of the children. They slept on blankets on the sand and washed in the oasis — or at least Nef did — and ate what the tribe did. They seemed happy, and it pleased me to see them playing with the other children without complaints or airs. I couldn't remember the last time either had mentioned palaces or servants, hot baths or soft beds, or that their older sister was the Queen of Egypt. Perhaps they were starting to forget they had once been princesses. I supposed children forgot quickly at their age.

Hennie, too, had settled into our desert lifestyle, although perhaps not as easily as the girls. Her old joints pained her at times and she found it difficult to get up and down from the sand. Still, she didn't complain and she seemed content enough. The girls called her Grandmother and if either she or they remembered she wasn't really, it didn't seem to bother any of them.

Our original plan had been to make a life for ourselves on the Red Sea coast. We would have fished and eaten eggs from the sea birds. I could still picture the little house I had intended to build for us. But it seemed I was the only one who wanted this, despite the promise of cool breezes and a more moderate climate.

The longer we stayed, the more restless I felt. It seemed unlikely the men searching for the missing princesses had given up. They got to Nef once and stole her away, presumably intending to take her back to Akhetaten where they would kill the queen and put Nef on the throne — with one of their own to act as regent, of course. Eventually, they would catch up to us again. The only thing I didn't know was when.

TWO
TEY

When the Sand Wanderers took us in, they quickly realised guard duty would suit me far better than spending my days cooking and minding the young children as the other women did. They tested me, of course, before they trusted me. Twice they sent men of the tribe to sneak up on our camp while I was on watch. I spotted them both times.

With the first, I had him on the ground before anyone could tell me it was just a test. I thought he was looking for the girls and it was only the memory of the farmer I killed for doing no more than watching us that slowed my hand long enough for him to tell me. When the second man came creeping in a few days later, I alerted the other guards in accordance with their protocols rather than taking him down myself. Either they didn't test me a third time or I failed.

After that, I took a regular turn at scouting with the men who watched over the desert surrounding us. Two of their number spoke Egyptian and they taught me their language as we travelled. After two years of living with the Sand Dwellers, I could converse well enough with them, although Hennie and both girls were more fluent than me.

Today we were patrolling a league in each direction around

the camp. The tribe was always on alert, watching for any sign of people nearby. There had been a time some years ago — a generation or more — when aggression between tribes was more common than it was today. The Sand Wanderers hadn't forgotten and kept close watch for anyone who might stray too close to their camp. Their diligence had proved fortunate for us when Seti ran away and a sandstorm hit while I searched for her.

While I was thinking, my gaze travelled over the landscape. Even though the scouts trusted me, I still felt like I had to keep proving myself. I spotted the men at the same time as Kashta, who was at the head of our party.

"Men," Kashta said. "Ahead and west. I count five."

"Egyptians," I added.

Their skin colour and their *shendyts* identified them as Egyptian, even if they wore shirts to shield themselves from the harsh desert sun and headscarves to protect their scalps. They rode donkeys as any sensible person would when venturing this far into the desert.

They were a rugged group and the way they carried themselves told me this was no band of mercenaries. These were trained men, professional soldiers, every one of them. My dagger was already in my hand as I studied them. Had men sent by Pharaoh's chief advisors finally found us again?

The Sand Wanderers made no effort to hide. Why would they? Everyone knew about the tribes living out here in the desert. Nobody cared, even if it was technically Egyptian territory. Few wanted to live in such a harsh environment and even fewer could thrive out here. Most Egyptians didn't have what it took. The heat of a city was nothing like out here in the desert, where there was no shade, only hundreds of leagues of endless sand. There were oases, if one knew where to look, but the Sand Wanderers kept their locations a closely guarded secret.

As the Egyptians approached, Kashta raised his hand in a friendly gesture. He was the only other scout in our party today who spoke Egyptian, so he would speak for us. I edged back a little, trying to position myself behind another of my companions. He leaned down to scratch his leg and took a step to the side as he did, which placed him more fully in front of me. His movement was so casual that I wasn't sure whether it was deliberate.

It was unlikely anyone would recognise me, dressed as I was in the manner of the Sand Wanderer scouts with a dark tunic, goat hide sandals, and a scarf over my head, but there was no reason to draw attention to myself. If the men knew enough to search the deserts for us, a woman travelling with the Sand Wanderer scouts might be cause for suspicion.

"You are a long way from the cities of the Two Lands, my friends," Kashta said as the Egyptians stopped in front of us.

"We are searching for two girls," one of them said, presumably the captain of this half squad. He dismounted, although the rest of his men stayed on their beasts. "We heard there was a Sand Wanderers tribe out here and we thought to enquire if you have seen or heard anything of them."

I held my breath, but Kashta didn't even so much as glance at me.

"I am afraid a couple of girls would not last long out here." Kashta's tone was amiable. "This is a harsh environment, friends. It takes much skill to survive in the desert."

"We don't believe they are alone," the captain said. "They must have guards with them. Egyptians, most likely. Well trained and capable of living out here."

"And who are these girls that are so important as to have guards with them in the desert?" Kashta asked.

"Princesses," the captain said. "Daughters of Pharaoh Akhenaten, may he live for millions of years. Sisters to Pharaoh Tutankhamun, the Strong Bull. Sisters also to Queen Ankhesenamun, Lady of the Two Lands. The princesses were stolen from the palace more than two years ago. The queen has charged us with finding them and returning them to their rightful place at her side."

Queen Ankhesenamun? The name was similar enough to that

of the girls' sister, Ankhesenpaaten, that I figured it was her he meant. She must have changed her name. And who was Pharaoh Tutankhamun? Was that the boy who used to be called Tutankhaten? The girls' younger brother, the one that was frail and not expected to live to be a man? So Pharaoh Akhenaten's heir must be dead and their sister had married their younger brother and made him Pharaoh. I studied the men, searching for any sign they were lying. Could it be true? Had the change of Pharaoh meant the queen had sent for her sisters? Did this mean it was safe for them to return?

"I am afraid we have seen neither girls nor guards out here," Kashta said. "What makes you think they are in the desert? Surely this is no place anyone would hide away princesses. The desert is vast, yes, but it is also inhospitable unless you know it well."

"We tracked them as far as Nebtu," the captain said. "We believe they travel with a woman, perhaps claiming to be their mother."

"So you think the desert hides princesses and a woman, as well as a squad of guards?" Kashta asked with a laugh. He sounded delighted with the conversation. "What else travels with them? Do you think they have a palace, ready to be erected on the sands when they stop for the night? Perhaps they carry tubs filled with perfumed water for the princesses to bathe in?"

Kashta knew, or at least suspected. He was an amiable fellow and I had never heard him be anything other than cordial to those we encountered while out scouting. He never said anything that could be taken as an insult, but it seemed he tried to offend the Egyptians. Maybe he hoped to dissuade them from accompanying us back to the camp?

What would I do if that happened? I could hardly run ahead to warn the girls to hide. I would have to trust they looked enough like the other children that nobody searching for a pair of missing princesses would look twice at them. They were not the only girls of their ages in the camp.

"We think it more likely they have fallen in with one of the tribes living out here," the captain said. "You haven't heard anything?"

"Nothing," Kashta said. "But then, it has been a couple of months since we last encountered another tribe. News does not move fast out here."

"We have been travelling for some days," the captain said. "We would welcome the chance to accompany you back to your camp and rest for a day or two before we move on. Would your tribe be willing to extend us some hospitality?"

"Of course." Kashta's voice was still easy. He turned back to the rest of us. "You three." He pointed to me and two of the men. "Go on ahead to tell the women to prepare extra food for tonight. Tell the men to ready shelter for the Egyptians. I am sending all three of you so you can help them. The rest of us will rest for a while before we follow you. My bad knee pains me today and I cannot continue until I have rested."

His gaze lingered on me no longer than any of the others, but I knew he intended this message for me. He still spoke in Egyptian, so the men we had encountered would understand, and he was well aware I was the only other one here who spoke the language. Also Kashta didn't have a bad knee and, despite his age, he needed to rest no more than the younger scouts. He suspected he knew who the Egyptians were searching for and he was giving me time to get them away.

As the three of us left, Kashta issued directions to the remaining scouts, telling them to get a fire going and cook the lizards we had caught so they could offer immediate hospitality to their guests while he rested his sore knee.

The two scouts had enough sense to hold their tongues until we were well away from the rest of our party, even though they would have understood nothing of Kashta's conversation with the Egyptians, or of his instructions to us, other than that he had gestured for them to go with me.

"What was that about?" one asked once we were out of both sight and hearing of the others.

"The Egyptians claim to be searching for two stolen princesses," I said. "They say they have been sent to find them and take them home. They also asked for hospitality from the tribe and Kashta has sent us on ahead to help with the preparations. He said he had a sore knee and wanted to rest before he followed us."

The man shot me a look.

"Interesting Kashta thought it necessary for three of us to go," he said.

"Indeed," I replied, careful to keep my tone indifferent. He must suspect, of course. Kashta's intent to delay the Egyptians would be obvious to anyone who knew him.

"They might be only an hour or two behind us," the other scout said. "That is not a lot of time to prepare for so many extra men. They will be eager for a good meal if they have been travelling through the desert for some days."

I said nothing, unsure of what he was trying to say.

"Perhaps we should hurry," the first man said. "The women will need as much time as possible to prepare the food."

As we jogged towards the camp, my mind was calm. I didn't know how the Egyptians had tracked us here, but it was clear the Sand Wanderers would help us.

Intef surely knew I wouldn't trust anyone who said the queen had sent for her sisters. If the situation back in Akhetaten had changed and she had truly summoned them back, it wouldn't be with a story about them being stolen. If the queen wanted to recall her sisters, Intef would be involved. He would send a message with the guards — something I would know came from him to tell me I could trust them. Without that, I had to assume these men were here without either Intef's or the queen's knowledge.

We slowed to a walk just before the camp came into sight, not wanting to alarm the guards with our hurry.

"Go prepare your daughters," one of the scouts said to me. "We will see to everything else."

"Thank you," I said.

He went to his wife, who sat on a blanket, grinding emmer into flour. She shot an unsurprised glance in my direction as he spoke, then called out to the other women who set about bundling up packages of supplies. Meanwhile, men filled water containers from the oases, while others prepared our donkeys penned nearby in the wooden structure we erected at each oasis for the tribe's beasts. They were the same donkeys we left Hennie's home with, although two had since died, leaving us with only thirteen.

"Tentamun, what is happening?" Hennie asked as I reached her. She was the only one who didn't have a cover name, although we always called her Hennie and never Henuttaneb. "Are we moving on already?"

"We need to leave," I said. "There is a half squad of Egyptians heading this way. Kashta will delay them as long as he can, but they intend to stay with the tribe for a day or two. We must be gone before they arrive."

"You think they are looking for the girls?"

"They said they are looking for the queen's sisters who were stolen from the palace."

"Maybe she has changed her mind?"

"If the queen has sent men to retrieve her sisters, my brother would have been the one to make the arrangements. If they bear no message from Intef, these men are not from the queen."

"I will go pack my things," Hennie said.

"Are you sure you want to come with us? The tribe would let you stay. You would be much more comfortable here."

"Of course I am coming. I wouldn't dream of being parted from the girls now."

"It won't be easy travelling. We will have to move fast to have any hope of losing them."

"Tentamun." Hennie looked me in the eye. "I love those girls as if they were my own granddaughters. You are not taking them away from me."

I gave her a small smile and shrugged.

"I just wanted to give you the chance to change your mind," I said.

"I know, my dear, and I appreciate the sentiment. But I am coming with you."

"Go get yourself ready then," I said. "I will find the girls."

Hennie hurried off to our shelter while I searched for Nef and Seti. I spotted them sitting at the edge of the water with a group of children.

"Neb, Sensen," I called. "Come here please."

They left their friends, although the slumping of their shoulders and the pace at which they came to me showed their reluctance.

"We need to leave," I said. "The bad men are almost here."

Seti scowled and crossed her arms over her chest.

"I don't want to," she said.

I knew she would be the most difficult. She always was.

"Do you remember what happened the last time they found us?" I asked. "They took Neb and she almost died."

"I don't want them to get me again." Nef's eyes brimmed with tears and she sniffled. "But I don't want to leave either."

"The bad men won't find us out here." Seti's tone was dismissive. "There is too much desert. They cannot track us here."

"They will be here in less than an hour," I said. "I spoke to them myself. Kashta and the scouts are with them right now. They will delay the bad men as long as they can, but they are coming and we must be gone before they arrive. They might take both of you this time. Or maybe you have been too much trouble for them and it is not worth the effort. They might just kill you and be done with it."

"They won't kill us." Seti turned her back on me and looked out at their friends. "The tribe will protect us. The bad men cannot kill us even if they find us."

"Sensen." I grabbed her shoulders and turned her to face me. "They will kill every person here if that is what they must do. Is that what you want? Your friends dead, their families dead. All because you refused to leave when the bad men arrived."

Sand swirled around our ankles despite the complete lack of breeze. She hadn't done something like this in months.

"If the tribe won't protect us, then I will." Seti's tone was defiant. "I can, you know. I have been practising."

"Sensen, you promised you wouldn't use your ability," I said. "What have you done?"

She waved her hand and the sand rose, swirling around us at waist height. She gestured and it sank back down to weave in and out around her ankles. I glanced around, fearing someone might have seen, but nobody was looking at us. They were all busy preparing for our departure.

"I have been learning how to control it," she said. "I needed to be ready for when the bad men came. So we don't need to leave. I will protect us."

We built a sand fort and hid inside it. That was what Nef said just the other day. I hadn't realised what she meant. It seemed the other children, at least, knew of Seti's ability. Fury rose within me, sudden and strong. Something about Seti triggered my anger so easily. I took a deep breath and pushed it away.

"We will discuss this later," I said. "Right now, we need to move. Go pack your things."

"No." Seti stomped her foot in the sand and glared at me. "I told you I don't want to go."

"And I told you we are leaving. You can either go get your things and get yourself on a donkey or I will put you there myself and tie you to it."

"I will scream if you do. The bad men will know exactly where we are."

"You do that, Sensen, and I will leave you behind for the bad men to find. Hennie, Neb and I are leaving. Come with us or don't." I nodded towards Nef. "Go, Neb. Get yourself ready to leave."

Nef hesitated, looking from me to Seti.

"Go," I said, more forcefully.

"Come on, Sensen," she said. "I don't want the bad men to get me again."

"They won't," Seti said. "I told you I will protect us."

"I think you might be too little," Nef said. "We need Mama to protect us right now."

"I don't want to go." Seti's fury seemed to disappear as quickly as it had come, replaced with misery. Her eyes filled with tears and she scrubbed them away with a dirty fist. "I don't want to leave my friends."

"I don't want the bad men to get me again." Nef reached for Seti's hand. "I was so scared last time. He was so strong, he didn't even notice me kicking and wriggling. I couldn't do anything and

I still dream about it. I dream he comes and finds me again. If the bad men are coming, I don't want to be here."

Seti still hesitated, biting her lip as she looked from Nef to their friends. I held my breath as I waited. It would be so much easier if Seti would come willingly. At last, she sighed and nodded.

"All right," she said.

FOUR
SETI

I grumbled to myself as I put my things in a pack. I didn't have much, just some clothes, a few necklaces and bracelets we had made in our lessons, and the three little wooden men I brought from Grandmother's home.

I liked living with the Sand Wanderers. There were no guards or tutors or nannies. Nobody telling me it was time to come inside or that I should learn to walk instead of run. I was nine years old now and Nef was ten, almost eleven. If we still lived in the palace and if our father hadn't gone to the West, he would probably already be thinking about who Nef would have to marry. In another year or two, she would be old enough for a husband.

Did the Sand Wanderers do the same thing? Did their girls marry old men who were useful to Pharaoh? None of my friends were married yet and nobody ever mentioned their father planning who their husband would be. I had never thought to ask. Maybe it was a good thing we were leaving. If we went to the coast and lived on the beach, like Tey had said we would, there wouldn't be anyone for Nef to marry. She and I could stay together and we could swim in the sea and play in the sand.

The bad thing rumbled inside me. It knew I was only

pretending I wanted to leave. I held my breath for as long as I could and when I needed to breathe, I did it real quick, then held it again. If I didn't breathe, the bad thing might not be able to come up out of my throat.

FIVE
TEY

The tribe worked together to prepare for our departure. As soon as we had packed our personal items, two men dismantled our hide shelters. The women assembled bundles of food and other things we would need, like cooking pots and mugs. A pair of older boys bundled up firewood. Men harnessed our donkeys and loaded them with our packs and skins of water.

There was no time for farewells. I caught the girls looking towards their friends who still played on the banks of the oasis, oblivious to our impending departure. I regretted we couldn't stay long enough for them to say goodbye, but the Egyptians might not be far away, and I feared Seti would change her mind if she had time to think.

The tribe's chief waited with our donkeys. Old Man was withered and stooped, seemingly ancient, but his mind was as sharp as ever.

"Thank you," I said. "I don't have the words to express what it has meant to us that you welcomed us into your tribe. Please tell them we are very grateful, both for taking us in and for your help today. I saw the supplies being packed for us and you have been most generous."

"You and your family will always be welcome with us, Tentamun." He handed me the donkey's reins. "I don't know what you flee, but I always suspected the day would come when you would leave us. Two women and two girls would not venture out into the desert alone unless their situation was most dire."

I nodded, but couldn't quickly decide what to tell him. Maybe it was best if he didn't know the truth about who we were. He could honestly tell our pursuers he didn't know his tribe had harboured the missing princesses.

"Go now, as fast as you can," he said. "We will keep the Egyptians well occupied while they stay with us, but I cannot control what direction they will go in when they leave. You must be well away before then."

"The supplies," I said. "This is a lot for us to take from what you have. We can pay you for them."

I reached for my pouch, intending to offer him one of the gems Intef stole from the girls' mother's collection, but Old Man stopped me with a curt motion of his hand.

"You are tribe," he said. "You do not pay for anything."

Hennie's bad knees made it difficult for her to get on her donkey, but a man stepped forward to help her. Others lifted the girls onto their beasts. I mounted mine and nodded a final thanks at Old Man.

"Go," he said, and slapped my beast on the rump.

As we set off, two women led a couple of donkeys on a winding path around the campsite. A group of children began playing a raucous chasing game, which seemed to involve kicking up excessive amounts of sand right where our donkeys had been standing. The tribe was covering our tracks.

If they could keep the Egyptians occupied for the rest of the day and through the night, hopefully the trail our donkeys left would be gone. The tracks would slide in on themselves and the overnight breeze would blow sand to cover whatever was left, along with any excrement the donkeys dropped as they walked. By morning, we would be far enough away that our pursuers wouldn't see our tracks.

I led us south. East towards the coast might be too obvious. After all, there weren't many places one could go out here. We couldn't head west, back towards Nubet, and north was the direction in which Akhetaten lay. I worried south might be almost as obvious as east, but this was what I had always planned to do when they found us again, and I wouldn't risk changing the plan without careful consideration. Go south for two days, then track east towards the Red Sea coast. I would stick to the plan.

Behind me, Seti sniffled, likely looking for attention. She knew the day would come when we would have to leave. I had told them repeatedly when we first arrived that we could only stay for a while. That sooner or later, we would need to move on.

Shortly after sunset, I drew my donkey to a halt.

"We will stop for an hour or two," I said. "Time to eat and rest the donkeys a little. I want to get as far away as we can before dawn."

Hennie climbed down from her beast with a groan.

"Oh my, these bones need to get used to travelling again," she said. She shot me a look. "Before you say it, dear, no, I am not sorry I came. I will get used to it in a couple of days."

"Can we have a fire?" Nef asked.

I glanced back in the direction of the camp, trying to estimate how far we had travelled. A league perhaps, maybe a league and a half.

"We are still close enough for them to see the smoke," I said. "Sorry, it will have to be a cold dinner."

"Never mind, dears." Hennie was already rummaging through the supply packs. "The women have packed us a fine feast here. Why don't I put together a meal while you girls feed and water the donkeys? They are the ones who have been doing the hard work this afternoon."

I trekked some distance back the way we had come, checking for any sign of pursuit. A bird called from high overhead. Nearby, something small scurried through the sand. Insects chirped. The breeze was light and absent of any trace of fire to indicate others were nearby. We were alone as far as I could tell.

How long could the tribe occupy the Egyptians? They might depart as early as dawn. We were safe enough for tonight, but once tomorrow came, I would assume they were following us.

I returned to the others and we ate. I slept for an hour while Hennie kept watch, then she woke me and I sat up so she could sleep for a while. We roused the girls and set off again.

SIX
TEY

We travelled south for two days, then turned east as I planned. When we first left Nubet, we travelled at night and rested during the day. But we didn't know whether anyone pursued us then. Since we knew men were definitely tracking us, I wanted to see them if they got close, so this time we travelled during the day.

The sun beat down relentlessly and the days were hot. The Sand Wanderers didn't track the months in the way we Egyptians did. The passing of the seasons was of little relevance to them. Out here in the desert, the days were always hot and the nights always cold. We were too far from the Great River to be affected by its annual inundation when the waters rose to cover the land. We saw no evidence of *peret* when the waters retreated, leaving behind the rich, black silt in which folk planted their crops. As resources in one area became depleted, the tribe moved to another oasis. That was the only season that mattered to them.

It might be *shemu* now — the harvest season. The days were not quite hot enough for the flooding months of *akhet*, but they were too hot and too long for *peret*. I supposed it didn't matter, though. As long as the weather was fine, which it almost always was, we could travel. We might be as little as a week from the coast.

On our second day travelling east, I woke early. Nef sat by the remains of our fire, head nodding. I rose from my blanket and stretched, then set off to make my usual circle around our camp, checking for signs of anyone nearby. To our west, a thin column of smoke drifted through the sky, likely the remains of an overnight campfire and perhaps no more than a league away. I ran back to our fire and smothered it with sand.

"Wake up," I said. "We need to leave."

Nef started and rubbed her eyes. She frowned at me.

"What is wrong?" she asked.

I pointed towards the smoke.

"If you had been awake while you were on watch, you would have seen it. We need to go before they catch up to us."

"Is it the bad men?" Seti clutched her blanket around her shoulders as she sat up. She yawned and scratched her head, tousling her hair, which already looked like a rat had nested in it.

"Why are you still in bed?" I snapped. "I don't know who it is. I know no more than you do, but someone is not far behind us and I don't particularly want to be here when they arrive."

Hennie, at least, had gotten up and was already packing our supplies. We had unloaded the donkeys last night to let them rest properly, something I now regretted as it would take far too long to load them again.

"We don't have time for this," I said. "Leave the rest. It might be better to travel light, anyway. If the donkeys are not burdened, we can swap between them more readily. We can go faster that way."

"You want to leave our supplies here where whoever that fire belongs to might see them?" Hennie asked. "Would that not signal more clearly than anything they are on the right path?"

"We can cover them with sand. It is unlikely they would stumble over the supplies if we bury them."

"So you want to head further into the desert with only a little food and water? And what do we do when that runs out if we haven't reached the coast yet?"

"We cannot be more than a few days from it."

"I think that sounds like a very good way for us to die out here." Hennie went back to loading up the donkeys. "How far away do you think they are?"

"Maybe a league."

"Then we can keep ahead of them. Their donkeys will travel no faster than ours."

While we were talking, the girls had shaken out their blankets. Nef stuffed her things into one of the donkey baskets while Seti just stood there and yawned, her blanket dangling from her hand.

"I am hungry," she said. "Can we have breakfast first?"

"We need to hurry," I said. "You can eat later."

"But I am hungry now."

I didn't respond. Hennie and I had almost finished loading the donkeys. I grabbed the last basket and Hennie helped me secure it.

"That is everything," she said.

"Tey, I said I am hungry," Seti said.

"Seti, get on your donkey. It is time to leave."

"I don't want—"

I glared at her.

"I am not going to tell you again," I said. "You can either get on your donkey and come with us, or I will leave you here for the bad men to find."

"You wouldn't do that."

"Try me."

Nef still stood beside her donkey and I shot a glare in her direction. She quickly mounted the beast. Hennie was already astride hers as I mounted mine.

"Let's go then," I said.

"Wait." Seti's voice was forlorn. "You wouldn't leave me here alone, would you?"

"If you want to come with us, get on your donkey now. I am not risking all our lives because you wanted a leisurely breakfast before we left."

Her lip trembled, but she mounted her donkey. I turned away so she wouldn't see my sigh of relief. The smoke had dispersed by the time we set off, although I could still make out faint trails of it. Whoever it belonged to was awake and had smothered their fire as they prepared to leave. If we pushed the donkeys hard enough, we should be able to stay ahead of them.

We travelled as fast as the donkeys could go. I felt bad there hadn't been time to give the beasts so much as a drink before we left, but if our pursuers caught up to us, it wouldn't matter whether the donkeys had drunk.

"Tey? I am really hungry." Seti's voice was plaintive.

I exhaled, trying to breathe away my annoyance at her, and didn't respond. Hennie told me once that the reason Seti annoyed me so much was because we were so alike. That we were both determined to get what we wanted, although we went about it in different ways. I tried to remember this when Seti annoyed the *ka* out of me.

"Did you hear me, Tey?" Her voice was louder now. "Nef, you're hungry too, aren't you?"

Nef murmured something I didn't catch.

"Grandmother, can you ask Tey when we will stop for breakfast?" Seti asked.

"For Aten's sake, Seti," I snapped. "Do you not understand we cannot stop right now?"

"But when will we be able to eat?"

"When it is safe to. You will not die of hunger in the meantime. You ate last night and you can survive until tomorrow, if necessary."

"Tomorrow?" Her voice rose. "I cannot wait that long. I am hungry *now*."

If she had been standing in front of me, I would have slapped her. It surprised me, this vicious urge that rose up in me from time to time. It wasn't that I actually wanted to hurt her. I just wanted her to stop whining. Had I been this irritating at her age? Dear Papa had never shown such impatience with me as I did with Seti.

Either I didn't annoy him quite so much, or he was better at hiding it.

Thank Aten for Hennie, who intervened just as I was about to get down off my donkey.

"Seti, you know we must hurry right now," she said. "If we stop to eat, whoever is following us will catch up."

"But Tey doesn't even know whether it is the bad men," Seti said. "It might be the tribe."

"I don't think that is likely, dear," Hennie said. "We know there are men looking for us. Remember, that is why we needed to leave the tribe. If someone is following, it is most likely them."

"Have you forgotten what happened last time the bad men found us?" I asked tersely. "They almost killed Nef. Do you want that to happen again? We might not be lucky enough to rescue her a second time. Or it might be you they take this time. Do you really want to risk it just so you can sit around and eat?"

Seti didn't reply, and I didn't look back to check why. I could hear her sniffling, even over the snorts and huffs of the donkeys and the noise they made trudging through the sand.

We reached an area where the flat plains became rolling dunes. As we crested the first, I looked back. Our pursuers were closer than I expected. If they had been a league away earlier, they had already made up at least half that distance. How could they move so fast? They must be travelling more lightly than us. They also probably hadn't wasted time this morning arguing over whether to sit and eat before they left.

I needed a plan. If we could see them, they saw us as well. They would move even faster now. Think, Tey. You need to be smart. There was nothing but sand for as far as I could see. Nowhere to hide and the coast was an unknown distance away.

If we could get to a village before they caught up, we would have a chance to find shelter. Or if the village was big enough to have a police chief, we could seek protection. We had a whole pouch of gems. Was that enough to convince the police to protect us? No matter how tenuous the plan, it was the only one I could think of. We had to get to the coast and find a village before they caught us.

"Hee yaw," I cried to my donkey.

He trotted a little faster, but already he breathed too heavily and his muscles trembled beneath me. The donkeys had walked a long way without water or a break. They wouldn't last much longer. We wouldn't make it to a village unless it was right on the other side of the next dune.

SEVEN
TEY

We crested another dune and this time there was no sign of our pursuers. Hope rose within me. Did we somehow lose them? Did they get disorientated and go off in a different direction? But at the top of the next, I spotted them again. They were closer now. Less than half the distance they were before.

My donkey came to an abrupt halt, jarring me from my thoughts and almost sending me flying over his head. A donkey behind us had collapsed, forcing the others to stop as well, since they were all tied together. I jumped down and sliced through the ropes tying the fallen donkey to the others.

"They are close, Tey." Hennie had dismounted as well, likely so she could speak to me without the girls hearing. "Do you have a plan?"

I tied the cut ends of rope together. It left two donkeys bunched too close, but there was no time to check whether anyone had thought to pack us some spare rope.

"I don't know what to do," I said. "Our options seem very limited."

"Should we leave the donkeys and run?"

"Where would we go? There is nothing but sand. We can only go so far without supplies and even less with the girls."

"What would you do if you were alone?" Hennie asked.

I looked around, considering. It was a good question. I hadn't thought about it like that. I had only been thinking about what I could do with the girls in tow.

"Hide," I said. "I would leave the donkeys and bury myself in the sand, hoping our pursuers would think I had fled."

"So we do that," Hennie said.

"I can help," Seti said. I hadn't noticed her approach. Nef, at least, was still on her donkey. "I can make the bad thing cover us with sand."

"No, Seti," I said, rather shortly.

"But I have been practicing." Already a whine crept into her voice.

"Seti, you promised you wouldn't use your ability. You don't know how to control it and it is too dangerous."

"But I can help."

"I said no. Now be quiet. I need to think."

Seti glowered at me, but I ignored her.

"We have been here too long," I said. "We have to move on."

"Seti." Hennie's voice held a note of warning and she was looking behind me.

I turned around. A sandstorm had risen, right where our pursuers were. Already I could see nothing through it, just sand whirling around them.

"Seti, how long can you hold it?" Hennie asked.

"I don't know," Seti said. "I have never done this before."

Had she forgotten the storm that sank the boat Nef had been hidden on? Or did she mean she hadn't tried to hold a storm for a prolonged period? It was too late to stop her and I could only hope she didn't hurt either herself or one of us.

"The donkeys cannot go on without rest," I said. "We will wait for a while if Seti can hold her storm. We should water the donkeys while we can."

I would have liked to offer the beasts some food as well, but by the time they had all drunk, Seti was already looking rather pale.

"We should go," I said to Hennie. "I am not sure she can sustain the storm for much longer."

"At least the donkeys have had a brief rest," Hennie said. "Perhaps that will give us the edge over our pursuers."

The donkey which had collapsed was unconscious. I couldn't leave the poor creature to die of dehydration or exposure, so I slit his throat. I gave him a brief pat on the nose and wished him well with whatever afterlife awaited a beast.

We helped Seti onto her donkey. I didn't speak to her in case she couldn't afford for her attention to be diverted from the storm. When we set off again, I considered going in a different direction in the hope of losing our pursuers, but our best chance of safety lay in reaching a village. So we continued east, although we didn't get very far.

"Tey," Hennie said. "I don't think Seti can keep the storm going much longer."

Indeed, as she spoke, a thud came from behind me. Seti had fallen right off her donkey. I jumped down and helped her sit up. Her face was a dreadful shade of grey and her eyes were far too bright.

"She has exhausted herself," Hennie said.

"Seti, let the storm drop," I said.

If she heard me, she didn't respond.

"Seti." I shook her shoulders. "Seti, you will kill yourself if you keep this up. Let go of the storm."

She still didn't respond. Fear made my hands tremble. We knew nothing about her ability. Was it possible that if she kept the storm going for too long, she could lose herself in it? Maybe she couldn't let it go? I shook Seti's shoulders again. Her head lolled to the side and she didn't seem to be aware of anything.

"Seti." I slapped her cheek and at last she stirred.

"The bad men," Seti whispered. "They will catch us."

"I will think of something," I said. "Just let the storm drop."

"The bad men."

"Seti, let it go."

"Tey, I think she has," Hennie said.

I turned to see the sand was settling.

"They will come after us again as soon as they uncover their beasts," Hennie said. "What are we going to do?"

"We have to leave the donkeys," I said. "They are too conspicuous. Get behind that dune and we will bury ourselves in the sand. They cannot miss the donkeys, but we might yet escape their notice."

I carried Seti, for she could barely stand, let alone hurry. When I thought we had gone far enough that our pursuers wouldn't stumble over us when they found our beasts, I stopped.

"Dig out a ditch with your hands, then lie down in it. Pull your tunic up over your head to keep some air and to stop the sand from getting into your mouth. I will cover you with sand. Keep absolutely still until I come to get you again. Understand?"

Hennie and Nef nodded, although both looked rather pale. Seti was still on her feet, but she wobbled and I expected her to fall over at any moment.

"Seti, do you think you can blow a little sand over our tracks?" I asked. "Just enough to cover the trail that leads from the donkeys to us."

Seti tried to speak, but nothing came out. Puffs of sand drifted over our tracks. Then she collapsed.

She still breathed, although shallowly. There would be nothing I could do for her if they found us, so I left her where she fell and dug out a ditch large enough for the two of us. By the time I finished, Nef and Hennie lay in their ditches.

"Pull up your tunic and hold it away from your face," I said. "Are you ready?"

They both nodded, although Nef was breathing far too fast. I swept the sand back over them, smoothing it as best I could so it looked natural. Nef was so small as to be hardly noticeable, but Hennie was a mound sitting a little above the surface. But the desert was full of dunes and one more small one would not be conspicuous. Or at least, that was my hope.

I brushed away my footprints as I returned to Seti, then lifted her into the ditch I had dug for the two of us. She didn't stir and I could only hope she wouldn't suddenly regain consciousness. She might panic and flail around, which would expose us. But it was too late to do anything else.

I pulled Seti's tunic over her head and tucked it in carefully so there wouldn't be gaps for the sand to flow in and choke her. Then I covered us over as best I could. Our mound undoubtedly wasn't as smooth as Nef's or Hennie's, but it was all I could do.

Then there was nothing left but to wait and pray to Aten that our pursuers wouldn't find us.

EIGHT

SETI

The bad thing was happy. I had never let it go like this before. Not even when Nef was taken. But the bad men had almost caught us and Tey thought they would kill me and Nef, so I told the bad thing to stop them from getting to us.

The sand swirled around the men, scraping their skin and pulling at their limbs. The bad thing would tear them to pieces. If they were dead, they couldn't chase after us anymore. I felt sorry for their donkeys, though. They would probably get ripped apart too. I didn't want the bad thing to hurt the donkeys, even if they were smelly and I didn't like them very much.

I wished I could see through the storm. Were the bad men scared? They should be. They had probably never seen anything like the bad thing before. I pretended I could see them. The bad thing was probably making the sand chase itself around the men. Over their heads, around their shoulders, between their legs. Over and under and around it swirled. The men got off their donkeys and made them lie down. Some of the men sat and pressed their faces into the beasts. Others dropped to their bellies and put their arms over their heads.

Maybe one man couldn't breathe. He had taken a mouthful of sand and it was down inside him. He would gasp and choke.

Reach out his arms, trying to find someone else in the storm. Someone to help him. But the sand would wrap around his arms and push his hands away so his fingers found nobody. He would fall to the ground and the sand would drape itself over his body so that even when the storm stopped, nobody would find him.

As the bad thing had its fun with the men, I started to feel very tired. One moment I felt well enough, but then the next I was so weary I could barely hold myself up. My limbs were heavy and my head nodded. My heart was having trouble beating. Maybe it was too tired to keep going.

I tried to stay awake. I had to get the bad thing back in my belly before I fell asleep. But the bad thing wouldn't listen to me and then I couldn't stay awake any longer.

NINE
TEY

We stayed buried in our sandy ditches for a long time. The sand was cool enough right now, but it would grow hotter as the day wore on. Hopefully, we would be out of here before it became unbearable. I had one arm under my tunic, which was drawn over my head and the other under Seti's tunic to keep her air pocket in front of her face. Her chest moved against me and her breath was hot on my arm. As long as she was breathing, she was probably all right. Or at least I hoped so. I could do nothing else for her.

When I was a child, Papa often bid me hide away and stay still for half a day or more at a time. He said it was part of my training, but I always thought he was just keeping me out from under his feet. For the first time, I understood the value of that particular exercise and I sent a silent prayer of thanks to Aten for Papa's forethought.

I strained to hear any noise that might indicate our pursuers were nearby. Was the absence of sound because the sand muffled it, or were they too far away? Eventually, I heard the braying of a donkey and voices, although I couldn't make out any words. They had found our beasts.

I heard nothing else for some time. Perhaps they left when they realised we were not with the donkeys? Then came a voice which was far too close. They were searching the area. Please Aten, don't let them come any closer. It would only take one man tripping over someone for them to find us all.

The sand shifted around Seti and me as someone walked right past. Voices. A lengthy discussion I couldn't quite make out. Then silence again.

I waited, hardly daring to breathe. The air grew thin and my head became dizzy. We couldn't stay buried much longer. Seti still breathed, although perhaps not as steadily as before. I tried to come up with a plan in case our pursuers were still in sight when we emerged, but my thoughts seemed to slide away. I was in danger of sinking into unconsciousness if I stayed in here much longer.

I dug my way out of the sand. I meant to do it slowly, so as not to draw attention in case anyone was nearby, but my heart pounded and my hands shook and suddenly I was desperate to get out. As soon as my face was clear, I gulped in mouthfuls of air. It smelled so fresh, I could barely stand it. My dizziness eased and my vision cleared. In my panic, I hadn't even realised I couldn't see. There was no sign of our pursuers. If they were out of sight, we had a chance to escape.

I uncovered Seti's face but left the rest of her buried while I rushed to Nef and Hennie. They were both dazed and flushed.

"Stay there," I whispered. "And be quiet. I am not sure they have left yet."

Hennie only nodded, but Nef whispered back.

"Tey, wait. What about Seti?"

"She lives," I said. "I can tell you no more. I need to make sure the bad men are gone before we deal with Seti."

I heard nothing from our donkeys, which were on the other side of the dune. The beasts were rarely silent, but perhaps they were too far away for me to hear their constant huffing and shuffling. There were no noises from our pursuers either. Hopefully that meant they had moved on. I crept around the dune.

Our pursuers did indeed seem to have moved on. And our

donkeys were gone too. If the men had killed the beasts, they would have left their bodies where they dropped, but I saw no blood and no donkeys, only sand, which was churned up and littered with excrement. The men had taken them and all our supplies.

Their tracks showed they had continued east. We had no choice but to go the same way — I wouldn't risk taking us deeper into the desert with no supplies — and would have to keep careful watch we didn't encounter them again. They might turn back or we might catch up to them if they rested long enough. But with no supplies, we wouldn't make it to the coast unless we were only a day or so away. I returned to the others, wondering how much to tell them.

"They are gone," I said. "It is safe for you to get up. Keep your voices down, though. They might still be nearby and you know how sound carries out here."

As Hennie and Nef shook the sand off themselves, I went to Seti. She seemed to breathe a little more strongly. I pushed the sand off her and my legs went weak with relief when her hands twitched and she opened her eyes.

"Seti? Can you hear me?"

Her gaze was unfocused and she didn't respond. At least she was conscious.

"Seti?" Nef crouched in front of her. She reached for Seti's hand and squeezed it. "Seti, the bad men are gone."

Seti didn't respond and Nef choked down a sob.

"Seti, please," she whispered. "Come on."

"Give her some time, dear." Hennie crouched beside Nef and put an arm around her. "She has exhausted herself."

I hadn't understood that moving the sand had a physical impact on Seti. It seemed obvious, of course, that such power must take something from her, but I didn't know. Perhaps she had gone too far this time.

I tried to remember how she was after the storm that sank the boat. A little tired perhaps, but nothing like this. Did Seti know her ability drained her energy? Maybe when she did something small, it was almost unnoticeable. Maybe she hadn't used it enough to understand, or maybe she knew but thought escaping our pursuers was worth the price. Her ability had saved us even as it nearly killed her, and that left me more conflicted about it than ever.

TEN
TEY

We could do nothing other than wait for Seti to recover.

"They are gone, I presume?" Hennie asked.

"East," I said. "And they took the donkeys."

"Our supplies?"

"Everything."

Hennie sighed and shook her head.

"I suppose it is too much to hope another Sand Wanderers tribe will find us," she said eventually.

"I cannot imagine we would be that lucky again. We will have to save ourselves this time."

"And how do we do that?"

"Continue east to the coast. We cannot be more than a few days away."

"A few days in the desert with nothing to eat or drink is likely longer than we can survive," Hennie said.

"I will think of something."

I got up and paced, suddenly unable to sit there and do nothing. The loss of our transport and our supplies was a heavy blow, worsened by the knowledge that it must have cost the tribe dearly to send us away with so many provisions.

"We will stay here until nightfall," I said. "Seti needs to rest anyway, and it will give them time to get far enough ahead. You and Nef should sit where the shade from your bodies will give Seti a little shelter."

I prowled around, watching for any sign of our pursuers returning. I followed their tracks for a way, but even when I crested a dune, keeping myself low to the ground in case they looked back, there was no sign of them other than the tracks leading ever eastwards.

Seti recovered as the day passed, although she made no move to sit up. As night fell, the air grew cooler.

"We should move," I said when my skin prickled with the cold. "We need to walk as far as we can before the sun comes up."

"Tey, I am thirsty," Nef said. "And hungry."

"I cannot do anything about that right now," I said. "But as we walk, look for plants and any sign of animals. If we can find something that lives out here, there will be water nearby."

Nef started to object, but Hennie stopped her with a few soft words.

The moon was only a half orb, but it was enough to light our way. It wasn't like there was anything to trip over, anyway. There was nothing but sand for as far as I could see. Many types of plants lived in the desert, though, and we would come across one eventually. When we did, I would dig down beneath it and hope to find water. As long as we had water, we would make it to the coast.

I kept a close watch on Seti as we walked. She stumbled from time to time. She needed more time to rest, but we couldn't afford to wait. We had to find water and we needed to get to the coast. Neither of those things would happen if we stayed here.

Seti's silence worried me far more than her complaints. I always knew she was well enough if she had the strength to whine. But as long as she could walk, we would keep moving. And I supposed when she could walk no further, Hennie and I would have to carry her. I didn't let myself think about what we would do when we no longer had the strength for that.

After a full day without water, we were weak and had to rest often. It was difficult to estimate distance in the dark, but I judged we had travelled less than a league. Nef stumbled and fell.

"Tey, we need to rest," Hennie said.

"I cannot walk any more," Nef said as Hennie helped her to sit up. She made no move to get to her feet. "I am too thirsty."

"We are all thirsty," I said, rather shortly. "I can do nothing about that until we find water."

"But I am really thirsty," she said.

I glared at Nef and she glared back. There was no point wasting energy arguing with her.

"Dawn is only a couple of hours away," I said. "We will rest here until then."

I took off my tunic and spread it over the sand. With luck, I might catch some dew and we could at least wet our mouths. Nobody asked why I was undressing, and I didn't have the energy to explain. I lay on the sand and fell asleep.

I woke shivering. We had nobody keeping watch. Our pursuers could have doubled back and found us. The others were still asleep. Hennie was curled up for warmth while Nef and Seti lay back to back. The sky was still dark, but a brightness in the east told me dawn was close. I crawled over to my tunic — it took less effort than trying to get to my feet — and found it had indeed caught a little dew. Not much, and it would dry quickly once the sun rose.

"Wake up," I said. "We need to go as far as we can before it is too hot to walk."

I wrung the liquid from my tunic into their mouths, Seti first, then Nef and Hennie, and the last for myself. There were only a few drops each, just enough to wet our tongues. Nowhere near enough to sustain us for the day. Tonight we would spread out all our tunics and perhaps we would catch more dew. If we lasted that long.

We walked a little way. Seti was still pale, but Nef looked flushed. When I pressed my hands against my face, my skin was hot and tight. My heart felt like it worked too hard and my breathing was ragged, even though our pace was slow. Despite the heat, I wasn't sweating, which worried me more than I wanted to admit. I forced my legs to keep moving. This was what I had trained for. I could push through it.

The world tilted and I found myself face down in the sand. It seemed like far too much effort to get up again. I managed to roll onto my side, but received a faceful of sand when Nef landed beside me.

"We will rest here," I tried to say, but only a groan came out of my mouth. I didn't try again. I didn't care whether they understood. It took too much effort to care.

The day was long and hot. The sun beat down on us and my skin burned. My tongue felt too big for my mouth and my throat was so dry I could hardly swallow. I rolled over at one point and found Hennie lying beside me.

"I don't think we are going to make it," I said to her.

She didn't respond.

ELEVEN
TEY

Night came eventually. There was something we were supposed to do. Something we had to do at night, but when I tried to figure it out, my thoughts slid away. It was easier to not think.

When I woke, the sun was well above the horizon and the air was already uncomfortably warm. My tongue was thick and sticky, and I couldn't swallow.

I had failed. Failed Intef and his queen. Failed the girls. Failed Hennie. I led them into the desert. Their deaths were my fault.

At least Intef would never know. Nobody would find our bodies out here. The sand would drift over us soon enough. The heat would preserve our corpses, and with our bodies intact, we could be resurrected in the afterlife. If we passed Osiris's judgement, we would go to the Field of Reeds. Perhaps I would see Intef there one day. I might have the chance to apologise.

After a time in which I knew nothing, I became aware of the heat and the sun beating down on me. The hot sand beneath my body. The harsh breathing of somebody beside me, although I didn't have the strength to lift my head and see who it was. My sky was so tight that if I moved, it would tear and fall right off me. It was fortunate I couldn't move anyway.

As the sun set and the air cooled, I woke. Had I been unconscious or merely asleep? For a while I lay there, too dazed to wonder what had woken me. I finally realised: the air had changed. It smelled fresher. We must be almost at the coast. Water might be only a couple of hours' walk away. We couldn't die here, not with the coast so close.

I managed to sit up, although my head spun, and it was a while before I could do anything else. Hennie lay on one side of me, Nef on the other. Beside her was Seti.

"Wake up." My throat was so dry, I could barely force out the words.

Hennie stirred and groaned, but didn't open her eyes. At least she was alive.

"Hennie." I raised my arm — Had it always been so heavy? How did I walk if my limbs weighed so much? — and shook her shoulder. "Get up. Almost there."

"Cannot," Hennie mumbled.

"Have to." So hard to force out the words. "Die here."

I shook Nef awake and somehow found the strength to get to my feet. I wobbled, the world tilted, and I stumbled a few steps, but didn't fall. By the time I had my balance, Hennie was sitting up. Between us, we got both girls on their feet. Seti was the hardest to wake. I knew she would be, although I couldn't remember why. My thoughts were slippery and wouldn't stay in my head long enough to make sense of them.

We staggered in the opposite direction of the sun. The sun set in the west. We wanted to go east. Had Aten sent the sunset to tell us which way to go?

We walked for no more than a minute or two before Seti fell. I hauled her to her feet and my head spun so hard I almost tumbled over on top of her. We stumbled on.

Nef fell next, and it took both Hennie and me to get her up again.

The sun disappeared and we had only the moon to light our path.

"Smell," Hennie mumbled.

It took a while to realise she had spoken and even longer to figure out what she said. I sniffed the air. Salt and freshness. I grunted. I had no words with which to reply.

I fell when my sandal tangled in the grass. I landed face first. Why did we walk when it took so much effort? It was much easier to lie here.

Something tickled my nose. I turned my head away.

Grass. Under my cheek. Cooler than the sand. Scratchy.

I lay there for a long time before I understood. I had barely enough strength to lift my head, but I saw the blades dotting the sand. Not very far away stood a shrub.

Plants meant water.

I tried to get to my feet, but I kept falling over. On my hands and knees, I crawled to the shrub, falling on my face just as I reached it. It was only then I remembered I wasn't alone. The others lay in the sand. Or they had fallen. Were they even alive? My limbs didn't have enough strength to carry me back to check.

With nothing but my hands, I dug down beneath the shrub. I was weak and the sand was heavy. It took a long time.

Damp.

Wet sand.

I dug further. Panting hard, I sat back on my heels to rest. When I reached into the hole again, my fingers touched liquid. Water seeped in.

I scooped some up in my hand. It was gritty and sandy, but it was wet. It was only a mouthful and my throat was so dry I almost couldn't swallow it. I dug down further and more water seeped in. I scooped up a handful and took it to Seti. Most of it had dripped away between my fingers by the time I rolled her over, but I trickled the rest into her mouth. She squinted at me, frowning as if she didn't know who I was. I left her there and took some water to Nef.

There wasn't much, just a couple of handfuls each, but it was enough to give us the strength to get up. We staggered on.

The moon was high overhead and a gentle breeze whispered

against my skin. Grass threaded the sand. More shrubs, and a looming shadow which was probably a dom palm.

Off to my left, a shrub rustled. There was something in it. An animal. We could eat it. I fumbled for a dagger, but dropped it and almost fell trying to retrieve it. I was too slow and made too much noise, and the creature, whatever it was, skittered away before I got anywhere near it.

I shook the shrub, hoping the creature might have left a mate behind, but nothing else came running out.

The others were ahead of me now. They didn't seem to have noticed I had stopped. Nef stumbled and landed on her knees. Hennie and Seti staggered on without noticing.

I reached Nef and grabbed her arm to haul her to her feet.

Ahead of us, Seti fell and didn't get up. Hennie stopped and stared down at her as if she couldn't figure out why Seti was lying down.

Water. We needed more water.

There was more grass here. More shrubs. And more water. I dug down below another shrub. The hole filled quickly. Still not enough, but more than before. After I had drunk a couple of handfuls, I finally thought to take off my tunic and filter the water through it. The others held their hands beneath the linen to catch the precious liquid.

"Cannot," Hennie said to me. "No walk."

It was all I could do to nod at her. None of us could walk further tonight.

The breeze was cold and we huddled together for warmth. Thoughts about starting a fire crossed my mind, but we had no flint and I didn't have the strength to sustain enough friction for a spark. The heat of our bodies would be all that warmed us tonight.

As more water seeped into the hole beneath the shrub, we took turns to drink. It still wasn't enough, but I could swallow without feeling like I would choke and my tongue seemed less swollen.

"Hungry," Nef moaned.

Hennie grunted, presumably an agreement.

As the sun rose, we each drank a little more, then we walked on.

I didn't notice the stream until Nef fell into it. It wasn't much — barely a couple of cubits wide and only a palm deep, but it was wet. Seti fell trying to reach for the water, so she lay on her belly and lapped it. I scooped some up and drank. My head cleared.

"Not too much," I said. "You will make yourself sick."

They ignored me and kept drinking. Hennie sat in the water, scooping it into her mouth as fast as she could. I dragged Seti back by her ankles, then hauled Nef out as well.

"Hennie, stop," I said. "You have to let your belly adjust first."

She stopped drinking, although she made no move to get out of the water.

"We are saved," she said.

TWELVE
TEY

We rested for a while, then we drank some more. My stomach cramped and I feared I had drunk too much too quickly, but it was probably hunger. How long had it been since we last ate? Two days? Maybe more. I had lost track of how long it had been since our donkeys and all our supplies were stolen.

I found a few tubers growing on the bank of the stream. I didn't recognise them and they weren't particularly palatable raw, but it was better than nothing in our bellies. As the sun reached its midpoint, we walked again, following the stream.

Our pace was slow and we stumbled often, but at least we had plenty of water. The stream grew deeper as we walked along its length and I spied a silvery flash within it. Fish!

It took much longer than it should have to catch two fish with my dagger. Hennie and the girls had been trying to start a fire, but they were too weak. I gutted the fish, then worked on the fire. That, too, took too long, but eventually a small fire blazed and our fish roasted on sticks. I found more tubers and set them to the side of the flames to cook as well.

My stomach cramped and grumbled at the aroma of roasting fish. We burnt our fingers and our tongues eating them half-cooked. The tubers were still mostly raw, but we ate them anyway. I drank more water and lay back on the grass. The fire warmed my feet and the air was filled with the soft trickling of the stream, the crackle of the fire, and the chirping of insects.

"We would not have survived were it not for you, Tey," Hennie said.

She poked another stick into the fire. The flames flared, then settled again. By the time I thought of a reply, I figured she no longer expected one, so I said nothing. I dozed for a while until I realised someone should keep watch. I started to sit up, but Hennie stopped me.

"Sleep, Tey," she said. "I will stay up. You have done enough."

I lay down again.

"Wake me when you get too tired," I said.

I was deeply asleep when Hennie shook my shoulder. She lay down and seemed to fall asleep immediately. I walked around for a bit, fearing I would fall asleep again if I didn't. I splashed some water on my face and drank deeply, still thirsty.

The sky changed from darkness to a brilliant orange as the sun rose. I left the others to sleep. There was no reason to hurry, and we were all fatigued and weak from hunger. I tried to catch another fish, but either they were too fast this morning or I was too slow. I found some more tubers and set them beside the fire to cook. At least we would have something in our bellies.

We followed the stream to where it ended in a shallow, rocky pool. The air was fresh and salty, with none of the heat of air warmed over scorching desert sands.

"What do we do now?" Hennie asked.

"Keep walking to the coast," I said. "We cannot be far away."

"You want us to leave the water?"

"We cannot stay here. There is no shelter, little food. We need to keep going."

"But what if we cannot find water again?" she asked.

"We will drink as much as we can. It is cooler here and we will last longer without water than in the desert. We will make it to the coast."

"We are still weak, Tey. It will take us days to recover."

"We will walk for half a day," I said. "If we don't reach the coast in that time, we can come back, but look around us. There are plenty of plants and that means there is water. We are in no danger of dying of thirst here."

Hennie pursed her lips and looked away.

"I know it is hard to leave the stream," I said. "But we have no other choice."

She didn't reply.

"Hennie, do you think I would suggest taking the girls away from the stream if it wasn't the only option? I would not deliberately endanger them. My task is to keep them safe. I cannot return to Akhetaten and tell my brother I failed by letting them die of thirst."

"And yet they nearly did."

"What would you have me do differently? They stole our transport and all our supplies. What happened after that was not a result of any decision I made."

She looked at me for a long moment.

"You think I was wrong to hide in the sand?" I asked. "Is that it? You think we would have been in less danger if they found us?"

"No," Hennie said. "Yes. I don't know. But if they captured us, they would at least have given us food and water."

"They would have killed you and me, and taken the girls. Do you think that would be better for them than the four of us being together? I know it was hard, but we survived. And now we need to keep moving."

Hennie sighed and studied the girls. They sat beside the stream with their backs to us and I couldn't tell whether they were talking or just sitting. Nef trailed her fingers through the water.

"All right then," Hennie said at last. "We will walk for half a day, but no more. If we haven't found water by then, we will come back here."

"Fine," I said.

There was no point arguing with her. If she didn't yet see we couldn't stay here, she would soon enough. Once we were away from the security of the stream, it would be easier to convince her to keep going.

The girls were less reluctant to leave than Hennie. Seti muttered about wanting a proper meal. She would keep moving forward if I dangled the possibility of food other than fish and tubers. Nef would likely go along with whatever Seti did, so it was only Hennie I needed to convince. If all else failed, I could simply refuse to bring them back. I doubted any of them would try to find their way here alone.

Our pace was slower than I liked and Seti soon lagged behind. My promises of food and water did little to hurry her.

I had a brief argument with Hennie around the middle of the day when she said we should turn back.

"Come on, Hennie," I said. "We are almost there. Can you not smell the change in the air?"

She glared at me with a stubborn expression so similar to Seti's that I had to remind myself she wasn't really the girl's grandmother.

"You promised, Tey," she said. "You said if we hadn't found water after half a day, we would turn back."

"But we are almost at the coast," I said. "Listen. I think that is the sea we can hear."

I had no idea what the sea sounded like, but I could hear a faint roar. It wasn't anything like the sound of the Great River, but maybe it was the Red Sea, which was far bigger after all. I couldn't imagine what else it might be.

I had tried over and over to picture the coast. Its shores were supposed to be sandy like the desert, rather than muddy like the Great River's, and I knew the sea was so big it stretched all the way to the horizon, just like the desert.

Hennie huffed. "I knew you were lying. You had no intention of turning back after half a day."

"What would we do if we turned back? Sit by the stream for

another day or two, eating whatever fish I could catch and any tubers we hadn't already picked, then try again? Do we walk all this way a second time and turn back again because we still haven't found water? We have no future unless we keep moving forward."

I kept walking and although I didn't look back, I could hear that all three still followed me. They had to. They couldn't survive out here without me. The roar grew louder until soon they could all hear it. When Seti complained her legs were tired and she needed to rest, it was Nef who urged her on with the promise that we must be almost at the coast.

I pushed through a row of dense bushes and there it was: an expanse of white sand stretching down to turquoise water, which I could only assume was the Red Sea.

THIRTEEN
SETI

I thought for sure we would die in the desert. Tey thought so too. I could tell from the look on her face when we saw the sea. She never expected us to get here. It made me mad to know she took us out into the desert when she didn't think we would survive. I did all I could to help — we wouldn't have escaped the bad men if I didn't send the bad thing to them — but Tey almost got us killed because she couldn't find enough water.

We should have stayed with the Sand Wanderers, like I wanted to. The tribe would have protected us. We didn't even know if there were actually any bad men coming after us when we left. Tey was the only one who saw them. The men who chased us through the desert mightn't even be the bad men. They might be looking for someone else.

We could have stayed if Grandmother and Nef didn't side with Tey. Nef should have sided with me. We were sisters, after all. Tey wasn't our mother, even if we had to pretend she was. She wasn't even related to us.

I wondered whether we could trust her, even though Nef said we wouldn't have lasted this long without her. But she did take us from the palace and the bad men said we had been stolen. Maybe when our sister let her captain take us away, she thought we were going somewhere else, but he gave us to Tey instead. Maybe we really were stolen.

I thought long and hard about this. Nef said our sister let the captain take us. That our sister trusted him. Nef trusted Tey, especially after the bad men took her and Tey found her again. But maybe Tey was the one who told the bad men where we were. Maybe it was her fault they took Nef.

The bad thing started rolling around inside my belly, like it always did when I got mad about something. I did some breathing, long and slow like Tey showed me. It seemed to help, or at least the bad thing calmed down and went back to sleep or whatever it did when it wasn't trying to get out of my belly.

Grandmother said we had to do what Tey said. That Tey was doing her best to keep us safe, Nef and me and even Grandmother. She was all sympathetic when it was just her and me talking, but when Tey was there, she always sided with Tey like Nef did. Nobody ever sided with me.

FOURTEEN
TEY

"Great Aten," Hennie muttered as she stopped beside me. "You did it, Tey."

I stared out at the water, speechless. It sparkled in the sunlight and I squinted against its brightness. It was true: the sea really did stretch all the way to the horizon, just like the desert did. Waves rushed away from the shore, only to turn and come back in again, arcing and curling over on themselves before splashing back down in a frothy white explosion. This close, their noise was deafening. The roar I had heard earlier was indeed the waves.

Nef squealed and jumped up and down.

"Can we go in the water, Tey?" she asked.

"Go ahead," I said. "Just don't go in too far. No further than your knees."

I had never had reason to ask whether either of them could swim, but I doubted it. Besides, even if they knew how to swim in the Great River, that would not prepare them for the Red Sea.

Nef ran down to the water and Seti mustered the strength to chase after her, despite her conviction that she was about to expire for lack of food. Nef stopped at the water's edge and waited for the waves to rush in over her feet. She squealed and danced back.

"It is cold," she called to Hennie and I.

Seti didn't hesitate, but ploughed straight in.

"Only to your knees, Seti," I called.

The water was mid-thigh on her and the current almost knocked her off her feet as the waves rushed out. She edged back towards the shore. Nef splashed her and Seti splashed back.

"Keep an eye on them," I said to Hennie. "Don't let them go out any further. I am not sure I can swim well enough to retrieve them if they get into trouble."

"Where are you going?"

"Over there." I pointed to where the sandy shore curved around out of view. "I want to see what is around the bend up there. I won't be long."

Hennie went to join the girls, and I set off. I discovered it was easiest to walk in the wet sand just below the top of the water line. The sand was cool and silky, and my feet sank, leaving perfectly formed tracks behind me. If we needed to escape pursuit here, we could avoid leaving a trail by walking through the water.

I rounded the bend to discover a pretty little inlet. The sandy beaches ended in rocky stretches which captured shallow pools of water. A crab scuttled away from me. It was too small to make much of a meal and I didn't know how we would get to its meat, but where there was one, there would be more. I made my way across the slippery rocks, studying the pools. A small fish was trapped in one and a strange orange creature with five legs in another. On one stretch, I found a row of shells which were stuck fast to the rocks. I pried one off with my dagger and discovered it contained a creature of some sort, slimy and salty but edible. Oysters maybe. I had heard of them, but had never tasted them before.

I made my way across the sand to where the vegetation began. The plants here were different from those I knew and there were few I recognised. A bunch of ripe dates dangled not all that far out of my reach. Using a stick, I knocked them down and gathered them in my skirt. If there was fresh water nearby, we could survive here. We could eat the shelled creatures from the rocks and whatever got trapped in the rocky pools as the tide receded. There were crabs and dates, and given the gulls wheeling overhead, there would be eggs as well.

I rushed back to share my discovery with the others. But when I rounded the headland, they were gone.

I shaded my eyes, hoping it was just the glare from the water that stopped me from seeing them, but they weren't there. I dropped the dates and ran to where I left them.

"Hennie," I called. "Nef, Seti, where are you?"

"Here," Nef called back.

I spotted them at last. They were up to their necks in the water. All three of them. Hennie grinned almost as hard as the girls.

"Come in, Tey," Nef called. "It is only cold for a moment, but then it feels wonderful."

"Come back," I said. "It is not safe to be out so far."

"Come and get us," she said teasingly.

"Hennie," I said. "You were supposed to be watching them."

"I am watching them," she said. "You know my eyes are not good and I can see them much better from here than from the beach. "

I hesitated, but if they got into trouble, it would be better to be out there with them than standing on the shore. I dropped my tunic on the sand, kicked off my sandals, and waded in.

A wave rushed towards me, shockingly cold against my thighs. As it flowed back out, it tried to pull me with it. I stopped and my feet sank in the sand to my ankles. Would I sink all the way down if I stayed here long enough?

When I reached them, Seti greeted me with a splash. They weren't as far out as I had thought and the water wasn't much deeper than my waist. I crouched down like the others so the water came up to my neck. Now my body had adjusted, the water was blissfully warm and I imagined I could feel it washing away the sweat and grime of the last few days.

"Don't drink it," Nef advised seriously. "It is very salty."

"I did, and it made my belly hurt," Seti said.

"No, it is not good for drinking," I said. "We will need to find fresh water."

"Will we stay here?" Hennie asked.

She cupped her hands and poured water over her hair. A wave caught Seti in the face and she shook her head, sending droplets splattering over us. Nef tried floating on her back, but another wave went over her face and she quickly righted herself.

"I want to stay here," she said.

"We will for a while," I said. "Until we recover. Then we can decide what to do. There is food here, and I am sure we will find fresh water as well."

"I would like to live by the sea," Seti said. "I am so sick of the desert."

I didn't remind her that a few days ago she wanted nothing more than to stay in the desert with the Sand Wanderers.

"It is very pleasant," Hennie said. "And I am sure we will be safe here. Who would think to look for us on an uninhabited beach?"

I ducked under the water and didn't reply. The men pursuing us would look everywhere. It would only be a matter of time before they found us again.

FIFTEEN
TEY

Although Nef shivered and Seti's lips had gone blue, it wasn't easy to coax them out of the water. Even Hennie was reluctant to get out. It was only the promise of food that finally got them all back to shore. I led them to the inlet I had found, collecting the dates I dropped on the way. We nibbled on the fruit as we explored.

The girls waded through the rocky pools, although Hennie was sure they would cut their feet to ribbons and insisted they keep their sandals on. We pried a dozen oysters off the rocks and set them aside for dinner. Nef found two small fish trapped in a rocky pool. With the fish, the oysters and another bunch of dates, we had enough to make a meal.

Once again, it took much longer than it should have to get a fire started. I was still weaker than I realised. If anyone found us tonight, I might not be able to fight them off.

"Tey, there is no need for you to frown," Hennie said quietly as we waited for the fish to cook. "We have food for tonight and a fire. Everything is well."

"We cannot stay here past morning." I glanced over at the girls again, even though I had checked on them only moments ago. They waded at the water's edge, and although I had sternly warned them not to go out any further, I didn't trust them to remember. "I have not found fresh water yet and we cannot go much longer without it. Not so soon after we almost died for lack of it."

"I admit I am rather thirsty, but we will manage for tonight. We have food, at least."

We were silent for a while. I watched the girls, and Hennie seemed to stare into the flames. I wished Papa was here. He always knew what to do. How to fix a situation, no matter how dire it seemed.

"Do you think there is a safe place out there for us?" I asked.

"I am certain there is, and I know you will find it, dear," Hennie said. "I would not have come if I didn't trust you to keep us safe."

"They will keep hunting us. They will keep coming until they get the girls."

"You won't let that happen."

I sighed and didn't respond.

"What is it, dear?" she asked. "It is not like you to be so doubtful."

"I am tired, I think. Tired of watching and waiting for them to find us again. Tired of waking up and wondering whether this is the day they will come. The day they will next capture one of the girls. Tired of fearing that if I let either of them out of my sight for even a moment, they will be killed."

"Did our time with the Sand Wanderers give you no reprieve from all that worry?"

"I still watched and waited every day we were there. I knew they would find us again eventually."

Hennie took so long to reply that I thought she wasn't going to. At length, she sighed.

"It is indeed a heavy burden you carry, Tey. I suppose things have not turned out as you expected when you fled Akhetaten with the girls."

The person I was back then seemed like a stranger to me now.

I had been filled with excitement at the thought of using my skills for something that mattered. Confident I would keep the girls safe. Success had seemed so inevitable that I hadn't even considered the possibility of failure. After all, I had spent most of my life training for something like this. Surely it was me the gods intended to shepherd these girls to safety.

But now I doubted myself. Doubted my skills. I had already lost Nef once and Seti almost died alone in the desert after she ran away. We all came perilously close to not making it to the coast. Would the next event be the one in which one — or both — of the girls died? Hennie's voice tore me from my thoughts.

"The fish is burning." She grabbed a couple of sticks and edged the rocks the fish lay on away from the fire. "Tey, let it go for tonight. Tomorrow, we will decide on our next move. But remember, you are not alone. There are four of us here and we can all share the burden."

The girls chattered as we ate, talking about what they saw in the rocky pools and how they looked forward to going back in the sea tomorrow. The air was cool and we huddled close to the fire for warmth. Seti was the first to yawn, although Hennie soon followed.

"Where will we sleep tonight, Mama?" Nef asked.

It was startling to hear her call me that. We had quickly fallen back into the habit of using our real names once we left the tribe, but maybe Nef said it without thinking. I couldn't imagine she actually thought of me as her mother.

"Here on the beach," I said. "We just need to make sure we are well above the waterline so we don't get wet with the high tide."

"It is too cold here." Seti frowned as she looked around, although I doubted she could see much past the patch of sand lit by the fire. "You said we would have a house when we got to the sea."

"We will," I said. "But we need to decide where to live and building a house takes time. It is not something I can do tonight.

We will sleep on the beach and put sand over us to keep us warm."

"I don't want sand all over me," Seti said. "It will make me itchy. I want a blanket."

"I am afraid we don't have any blankets." I fought to keep my tone steady. Considering her affinity with sand, I might have expected she would take to the idea of sleeping in it more easily. "A blanket of sand is the best we can do for tonight."

"I want a hot bath." Seti crossed her arms over her chest and glared at me. "You promised we would have beds and hot baths."

It had been so long since she last mentioned living in a palace that I thought she had forgotten she used to be a princess.

"We will," I said. "Just not tonight."

She opened her mouth, but I shot her a glare. Hennie spoke before either of us could say anything else.

"I have never slept on a beach before," she said in the bright voice she used when she sensed an impending argument. "Won't that be exciting? I cannot wait to nestle down into the sand. I think I will pretend I am some sort of burrowing animal and the sand is my den."

"Like a sand rat?" Nef asked. "I thought I saw one earlier."

"Ew," Seti said. "I hope it doesn't chew my feet while I am sleeping."

"Or maybe it was a crab," Nef said. "It might grab your toes with its pincers."

Seti looked a little pale.

"No, it wasn't a crab," Nef said. "It was a *sand flea*." She shouted the last and flung a handful of sand at Seti. "And it will crawl all over you while you sleep."

"Nef, enough," I said. "There are no rats or crabs or fleas in this part of the beach."

"Seti's toes got eaten by a sand rat," Nef chanted. "Seti's got sand fleas. Ooh, I bet you are itchy."

Tears welled in Seti's eyes, and she scratched her scalp.

"Mama, I have fleas in my hair," she cried.

"Seti, you don't have fleas," I said. "Nef, stop your nonsense. You won't be going in the sea tomorrow for teasing your sister."

Nef got to her feet and stomped away, kicking up the sand as she went. I sighed and started to get up, but Hennie stopped me with her hand on my arm.

"I will go," she said. "You stay and talk to Seti."

Seti pulled her knees up to her chest and wrapped her arms around them. She sniffed loudly, the noise she made when she wanted attention and sympathy.

"Seti," I said.

I stopped and sighed. Was it easier when the children came from your own body? I was fond enough of the girls after living with them for more than two years, but I wasn't sure I could honestly say I loved them and I never for a moment forgot I wasn't their mother. Did they still remember their mother? Did they even remember I wasn't her?

We never talked about any of their family. Perhaps that was a mistake. Maybe I should have encouraged them to speak about their mother and their father, the great Pharaoh Akhenaten, may he live for millions of years. Their sister, who was the Queen of Egypt, and their little brother, Tutankhaten, who now sat on Pharaoh's throne and called himself Tutankhamun. I hadn't even had a chance to share this news with them.

I had thought it best if they forgot they used to be princesses. That they once had palaces and jewels and servants to fulfil their every whim. They would never live like that again and I had thought remembering that life would make them resentful, but perhaps I was wrong. Maybe if I was really their mother, this would be easier. She wouldn't get things like this wrong. Seti's voice tore me from my thoughts and I realised she hadn't forgotten I wasn't her mother after all.

"Tey." Her voice trembled. "Why do you hate me?"

"I don't hate you." I was so surprised, I couldn't even think of what else to say. "Whatever gave you that idea?"

"You get so angry with me. You never talk to Nef like that."

I smoothed the sand around me while I tried to find a reply.

"You frustrate me," I said at last. "But I have never hated you and I am sorry I made you feel that way."

She didn't answer, only shrugged a little, and kept looking out at the water.

"I never wanted to be a mother," I said. "Have I ever told you what I wanted to be when I grew up?"

"Maybe," she said.

I half remembered Nef asking about my life on our journey down the Great River. Before we reached Nubet and found Hennie. A long time ago.

"I wanted to be a foot soldier, like my father," I said.

"Girls cannot be soldiers."

"I know. Everyone knows. But it was the only thing I ever wanted."

"Didn't you want a husband?" Her voice had lost its tightness now, and she sounded genuinely curious.

"No. Once a woman has a husband, she is expected to stay at home all day and look after things there. Direct the servants if her husband is wealthy enough to have any. Otherwise, she spends her days cleaning and baking bread and brewing beer. Then once she has children, she also has to look after them all day. I would..." I paused, trying to find the right words. "I would go out of my mind if I had to live like that."

"But you could still have a job," Seti said. "Don't lots of women work as... I don't know, maids or sewers or something."

"And they still have to clean and cook and brew beer and look after the children as well as do their job. They get worn out and eventually they drop dead from exhaustion."

"Really?" Seti gave me a wide-eyed stare. "I don't want to drop dead from exhaustion when I get married."

"You don't have to marry," I said. "Not if you don't want to."

"Of course I have to. Everyone does."

I sighed.

"Seti, I don't know how else to explain it to you. I am... different. I have always felt different. I don't want the things other women do."

I had always felt like I was meant for something more than just keeping some man's house and raising his children. Something big and magnificent and important. When I learned the queen's sisters needed to be taken away and kept safe, I jumped at the chance to take them. I had thought this was the thing I was waiting for. The big, magnificent, important thing. But now I wasn't so sure. I felt like I had trapped myself in exactly the life I wanted to avoid. And there was no way out.

SIXTEEN
TEY

Between Hennie and me, we calmed both girls enough that they finally went to bed, although not without much grumbling about the sand and the lack of blankets. I stayed up to keep watch, staying as close to the fire as I could. Around the middle of the night, Hennie came to sit beside me, shaking the sand off herself.

"Go get some sleep," she said. "I will sit up. I am too cold and my old bones would appreciate being by the fire."

I left her to it and burrowed down into the sand, but Hennie was right that it was too cold to sleep. I lay there for a couple of hours, but eventually returned to the fire. Hennie didn't speak when I sat beside her and she didn't seem inclined to leave the fire's warmth. Her head drooped and she seemed to doze.

As dawn broke, I went to wash my face in the sea. The cold water refreshed me and chased away my sleepless night. We needed to find shelter today, or at least a village where we could trade for some blankets. I doubted any of us were keen to spend another night buried in the sand.

I pried a couple of handfuls of oysters off the rocks and turned up the bottom of my tunic to carry them. We needed a change of clothes — my tunic would reek after being wrapped around the oysters. A pot or two for cooking and to carry water. Bowls and mugs. There wasn't much else we needed immediately. I eyed a row of palm trees not far from the shoreline. If we couldn't get blankets today, perhaps I could create some sort of shelter. A few straight branches, some palm leaves, maybe a length of vine to hold it together. It would at least provide some cover from the breeze overnight.

My mood was low as I trudged back up the beach. It would be so much easier to provide for only myself. Even making a shelter for one person was much simpler than making something big enough to accommodate four. When I left Akhetaten with the princesses, I had trusted my skills would be enough. But I hadn't understood how difficult it would be to survive when more lives than just my own relied on my abilities.

I dropped the oysters in the sand beside Hennie.

"Where are the girls?" I asked.

"I sent them to find some dates. They will probably be too high for the girls to reach, but they can at least show us where they are. It will be good for them to feel like they are contributing."

"I will go see if they have found any."

I already felt bad and didn't need Hennie pointing out the ways I could do better.

By the time I found the girls, they had not only located some dates, but had managed to knock down a bunch and were carrying it back between them. Mindful of Hennie's comment about them contributing, I didn't offer to help. They chattered about things they saw while they searched for the dates, last night's tension seemingly forgotten, and Seti complained briefly about a sore foot.

I was still hungry after I had eaten my share of oysters and dates. We needed to find something more substantial for tonight. I had nothing other than my daggers with which to fish, but I might find some sea bird eggs and there would be more of those tiny crabs and perhaps even other creatures burrowing in the sand along the water's edge. For now, though, our priorities were fresh water and shelter.

"We will walk along the shore today," I said as we collected the empty oyster shells and tossed them into the fire. "We need somewhere more sheltered to sleep."

"How far do we have to walk?" Seti's face had that calculating look that usually meant trouble.

"Until we find something suitable."

"But how far? We have spent days walking and my foot hurts."

"I don't know, Seti. I have never been here before. We will walk until we find shelter. That might be a cave or it might be a village. I don't know what is further along the shore, and the only way we will find out is to walk there."

"Maybe you could walk and we can wait here," Seti said. "I need to rest."

"We will all walk." My tone was curt now.

"Nef wants to stay here, too," Seti said. "Don't you, Nef?"

Nef looked between me and Seti, and for a moment I thought she would disagree, but then she nodded.

"I am pretty tired," she said. "I think Tey should go without us."

"We will all go and that is that," I said.

"But—" Seti started.

I glared at her, but Hennie spoke first.

"This will be such an adventure, won't it, girls? Walking along the seashore, looking for somewhere to live. I cannot wait to see what we find along the way."

With much huffing and puffing from Seti, we set off. She soon lagged behind, probably waiting for me to comment so she could tell me again about her sore feet.

The air quickly lost its early morning coolness, although the breeze sweeping in from over the sea kept us from getting hot, even as the sun climbed higher. We stopped to rest in the middle of the day. Seti sat on her own and refused to come any closer, even when Nef called her over. I avoided looking at her. She needed little encouragement to continue with such nonsense, and I was determined she wouldn't get any from me. My mouth was dry and despite the cool breeze from over the water, my skin felt hot and tight again. We needed fresh water.

Around midafternoon, we reached the end of the sandy beach and the start of a more rocky stretch of coastline. There were numerous rock pools filled with water and sometimes a small fish or crab or some other creature. Nef found a large slug-like thing that Hennie thought might be a sea cucumber. Whatever it was, it was definitely an animal of some sort, and I figured that meant it was edible. As we scrambled over the rocks, I spotted a nest. Inside were three eggs. I took two, leaving one for the birds that owned the nest. The eggs, sea cucumber, and a few little crabs or whatever we found in the rock pools wouldn't be much of a meal, but at least we had food for tonight.

"Where is Seti?" Hennie asked.

I couldn't see the girl anywhere.

"Seti?" I called.

No answer.

"Nef, when did you last see her?" Hennie asked.

Nef was crouched to examine a rock pool. She shrugged as she stood.

"A while," she said.

Unease rose within me. Had someone found us and been following and I hadn't even noticed? Had Seti been snatched while she trailed behind?

"Stay calm, Tey." Hennie must have sensed my growing fear. "If something had happened, Seti would have called out. She wasn't so far behind that we wouldn't have heard her."

I just shook my head and started back the way we had come. I didn't call out again. If someone had grabbed her, I didn't want to give them any warning of my approach. The rocks were slippery, and I slid, landing heavily on my hip. I made myself move more slowly after that. If something had happened to Seti, I couldn't help her if I was injured.

As I rounded a curve in the shoreline, I saw her. She sat on the rocks, her legs pulled up to her chest and her head resting on her knees.

"Seti," I said as I reached her. "What in Aten's name are you doing?"

She raised her head, and it was only then I realised she was crying. I crouched beside her.

"What is wrong?" I asked. "What happened?"

She hiccuped and pointed to her foot.

"I told you my foot hurt and you didn't listen. I walked as far as I could, but it hurt too much once we got to the rocks. I couldn't keep walking and I thought..." She hiccuped again. "I thought you would notice I wasn't there, but everyone kept going and left me alone."

I lifted her foot and brushed off the sand. Blood oozed from a long cut through the ball of her foot.

"Why didn't you tell me you had hurt yourself?" I asked.

"I did," she said. "You didn't listen."

I took a deep breath and tried to push down my irritation. I had thought she was just being precious — her old "I'm a princess and I cannot walk on my own feet" routine. Hennie told the girls to keep their sandals on. Of course, it would be Seti who disobeyed. Her sandals must be in her pack.

"I didn't know you were injured," I said. "Come on, I will carry you."

"Nobody even noticed I wasn't there."

"We did notice, Seti. We have been looking for you."

"Really?" She gave me a hopeful look.

She didn't need to know we had only just realised she was missing.

"I came looking for you as soon as we realised you weren't behind us."

"Did you think the bad men had found me?"

I didn't like the calculating tone in her voice. If I said yes, she might do something even stupider next time, like hide away to make us think she had been taken.

"I knew they wouldn't get to you without me hearing," I said. "Come on, up you get. That is it. Now, can you get onto my back? That will be the easiest way for me to carry you."

"Will you carry me until we find somewhere to sleep?"

"No, I will only carry you back to the others. Then we will wrap your foot and you will be able to walk."

I was tempted to wrap her foot here and make her walk, but she was in a mood and the quickest way to get her to come with me would be to carry her.

"I don't think I can walk any further today," she said.

"Let's see how you are once we clean up your foot."

My hip was still sore from my fall, so our progress was slow. Hennie and Nef were watching for us and as we came into sight, Nef started towards us.

"Seti, where were you?" she called once she was close enough.

Seti started crying again and didn't answer.

Nef patted her back as we made our way to Hennie.

Hennie looked from me to Seti and sighed.

"Come now," she said as I crouched to let Seti off my back. "What trouble have you got yourself into?"

Seti was heavier than I expected and my thighs shook from the effort of carrying her through the sand. I stretched my legs, trying to ease my muscles.

"She has a cut foot," I said, somewhat shortly.

I used a dagger to slice a strip off the bottom of my tunic and wrapped it around her foot. The cut wasn't all that deep, but blood still oozed from it.

"Can she walk?" Hennie asked. "I do not relish the thought of another night pretending to be a sandworm."

"She will be fine," I said.

"I cannot walk any more today." Seti's voice trembled a little too much. Now she had the attention she wanted, she would do what she could to keep it.

"If you cannot walk, we will have to sleep in the sand again," I said. "If you want to find shelter, maybe even some blankets, we have to keep going. You can rest a little, then we need to move on."

"You are not listening to me, Tey," Seti said. "I told you my foot hurt and you didn't listen. I told you I cannot walk any more and you won't listen to that either."

"Because the cut is not so bad that you cannot walk," I said. "You need to stop thinking about yourself and think about the rest of us. Nobody wants to sleep out here in the sand again tonight, but that is what we will have to do if you insist on pretending you cannot walk."

"Tey, dear." Hennie's voice was low and intended only for my ears. "Perhaps you should take a short walk? Calm yourself and then we can figure out what to do."

I opened my mouth, but snapped it shut again. It wasn't Hennie's fault Seti was so annoying. Indeed, if she wasn't here to mediate between us, I would probably lose my temper with the girl much more often than I did. Why had I thought taking charge of two spoiled princesses would be an adventure?

SEVENTEEN
SETI

My foot felt a little better once Tey wrapped it. I had cut it on the sharp edge of a fallen palm leaf while Nef and I were looking for dates earlier. Nef stayed close as Tey wrapped my foot, darting in to pat my shoulder or give me a quick hug. Grandmother gave me a sympathetic look even as she tried to convince Tey to stop being so mean.

It wasn't my fault Tey had to pretend to be our mother. I tried not to think about the before life because it made me sad. Back when we were princesses, we had everything we wanted, although I was starting to forget what those things were. It had been a long time since Tey took us away from the palace. She probably thought we had forgotten we used to be princesses, but I hadn't.

Father used to tell me I would have an important marriage one day. I didn't know how that would happen anymore. Who would choose a husband for me when I was old enough? Who would make sure he was a man who would be useful to pharaoh? But Father wasn't pharaoh anymore. He had gone to the West and maybe the new pharaoh didn't need men who would be useful to him. Everyone knew princesses were supposed to have important marriages. What use was I to anyone without that?

The things Tey said last night about not wanting to get married and drop dead from exhaustion confused me. I would have liked to ask her about it, but she would probably get angry with me. She might say she had already explained and I didn't listen properly. But I thought women were supposed to get married and I didn't understand why Tey said she didn't have to.

While I was resting and thinking, Tey went down to the water by herself. She just stood there on the edge of a rock and looked out at the sea. Maybe she was thinking about swimming away. I wouldn't be very sad if she did. There would be nobody to be mean to me if she went away.

Thinking about Tey leaving made my belly hurt. Who would protect us when the bad men came again? Grandmother was too old and Nef and I were both too little to fight the bad men, even though we were bigger than we used to be. Tey had taught us how to get away if someone tried to grab us, but I knew it wouldn't work because I was too little. If she was just a little nicer to me, I wouldn't mind her so much.

After a while, Tey came back and I let out a really big sigh of relief. She wasn't going to swim away and leave us after all. I thought she might say she was sorry for being so mean and making me walk so far, even though I told her my foot hurt, but she didn't look at me. She just said it was time to keep walking.

I was so angry with Seti that I didn't trust myself to look at her. We set off along the shore again, although not without a lot of fussing from Seti, who walked with an exaggerated limp. I felt bad for not realising she was injured, but it was her own fault, really. If she didn't whine constantly, I might take her complaints a little more seriously.

The shoreline was still rocky. It wasn't as nice as the sandy beach, but it made me hopeful we might find shelter. Indeed, we had only been walking for an hour when Nef called out.

"Tey, I found a cave," she said.

We all hurried over to look. Seti even forgot to limp.

Nef had indeed found a cave, although it was too small. It might fit one person comfortably enough, but not four.

"Good job, Nef," I said. "I think it is too close to the water, though. Look at that line of salt on the rock above it. It looks like this cave gets submerged when the tide rises."

"So we cannot sleep in here?" Disappointment tinged Nef's voice. She badly wanted to be the one to find us shelter.

"I am afraid not." I patted her shoulder. "We need a cave that is a little bigger and is further back from the water."

We continued walking, with Nef hurrying ahead in search of a better cave. Seti tried to keep up with her, but soon dropped behind again. She limped a little, not the exaggerated limp of earlier, but a real one. I hardened my heart. Our need to find shelter was greater than Seti's need to rest her cut foot. Once we found somewhere to sleep, she could rest all she wanted.

When Nef next called out, I expected to see another small cave. But she disappeared inside while I was still on my way to her. I broke into a run.

"Nef," I called. "Wait. You don't know what is in there."

Thoughts of wild cats and cobras and nests of scorpions ran through my mind as I raced to the cave. The entrance was not much bigger than a man, but it opened up into an area about the size of Hennie's cottage.

"Is this one good?" Nef's voice was hopeful and she clasped her hands together as she waited for my response.

"Yes, Nef, this is very suitable."

I had hoped to find a cave with a natural opening at the top for smoke to escape from, but that was the only thing it lacked. We wouldn't be able to have fires inside, but it was plenty spacious and far enough back from the water that we wouldn't need to worry about the tide. It was cold, though. I had no experience with caves, but the one time I had been inside a tomb in the rocky cliffs that surrounded Akhetaten, the air was hot and the rocks warm to touch. I had expected a cave to be the same, but these rocks were cold and my arms were already pimpled with goose-bumps. This would give us shelter, but we definitely needed blankets.

"Oh, this is wonderful." Hennie wrapped her arm around Nef and squeezed her shoulders. "Well done, dear."

A sniff from Seti drew my gaze to her just in time to catch the glare she shot Hennie and Nef. Was it Nef's find or Hennie's praise that had upset her now? Tension between the girls was the last thing we needed.

"It is cold in here," Seti said. "And we don't have any blankets. I think we should find a better cave."

"Seti, dear, Nef has found us a wonderful place," Hennie said.

Hennie had more experience with children than I did, so if she thought ignoring Seti's mood was best, I would do the same.

"I think it is perfect," Nef said, seemingly oblivious to Seti's glower.

"I will look for a village tomorrow," I said. "There will surely be a number of them along the coastline, so I will walk until I find one. For today, let's make sure there is fresh water nearby. We cannot stay here otherwise. And I want to make sure you have a couple of days' food before I leave."

"Come on, then." Hennie's voice was filled with enthusiasm she undoubtedly didn't feel considering we had already walked for several hours today.

It took only a few minutes to find a creek that emptied into the sea. When I tasted the water, it was fresh with no hint of salt. Nef copied me, cupping her hands to drink from the creek.

"It tastes sweet," she said.

"The water must come from a river further upstream," I said.

"It is not very big." Seti's voice was doubtful. "I cannot bathe in that."

The creek was only about a cubit across.

"We will bathe in a bucket," I said. "It is plenty big enough to provide enough fresh water for our needs."

"We don't have a bucket," Seti said.

"I will get one when I go for supplies," I said. "In the meantime, I will make a couple of bowls you can use to collect water."

"I cannot bathe in a bowl."

She sounded scornful now, and I bristled. Hennie must have sensed my rising irritation.

"No, you cannot," she said in the cheerful voice she used when she was trying to avert a conflict between Seti and me. "But we have drinking water and you can splash yourself in the creek if you must bathe before Tey returns with a bucket."

Nobody commented on Seti's unusual dedication to bathing.

Considering she never bathed until someone reminded her at least twice, she was looking for things to grumble about.

While the girls searched for ripe dates, I looked for anything else edible. I had hoped to find some tubers, maybe even a fig tree, but other than a sage bush, there was nothing else I was sure was safe for us to eat. The girls found several dom palms with large bunches of dates that were only a couple of days off being ripe. To my relief, Seti located two herself, which pleased her immensely and she seemed to forget her jealousy that Nef had found the cave.

Down at the shoreline, we found an area of rocky pools only a short walk from the cave. That, at least, provided more food than the vegetation. There were oysters and several tiny octopuses. An abundance of little crabs scurried across the sand, so it seemed they would be a large part of our diet, at least until I could get a vegetable garden growing. I would have to get seeds — cucumber, lettuce, onion, perhaps some melon. Maybe we could even grow our own emmer.

It dismayed me to realise how many things we needed to eke out even the most basic existence. It was much more than the blankets, change of clothes, bowls, buckets and cooking pots I had envisioned. Food, it seemed, would be our biggest problem. A diet of baby crabs, oysters and dates would keep us alive, but it would quickly become monotonous. We needed bread and vegetables. We could manage without beer since we had fresh water, but I toyed with the idea of a goat. If we had milk, we could make cheese to provide some variety in our diet, but a goat needed food and that would make the problem of supplies even bigger.

"You look troubled, Tey," Hennie said quietly.

I had been so absorbed in my thoughts, I hadn't noticed her come up beside me as I stared out at the ocean.

"Worrying about how we will feed ourselves," I confessed.

"I have to admit, I thought there might be more food around

us. I suppose I am too used to going outside and picking whatever is ready in the garden."

"We will make a garden, but crops take time to grow and it will be hard work to feed ourselves until then."

"Perhaps there is a village not all that far away," she said. "You are worrying unnecessarily. If we can access supplies with just a few hours' walk, we will cope well enough."

"Let's not make any firm decisions about staying here until we know how far the nearest village is. If I cannot find one within a day's walk, we need to look for somewhere else to live."

"It will be fine, dear," Hennie said, patting my arm. "You will see."

NINETEEN

TEY

I spent the rest of the day carving a couple of bowls from driftwood I found on the beach. Although my daggers were sharp, they weren't really suited to such a task. A good knife was another thing I needed to get when I went for supplies.

The girls busied themselves dragging palm leaves into the cave and figuring out how to weave them together. It was Nef's idea, still buoyed from being the one to find us a cave and eager to show how else she could contribute. Seti helped, although with obvious reluctance. The blankets they made were awkward, and I doubted they would do much to keep us warm, but they would be better than nothing and at least the girls were trying. We used my new bowls to bring in sand to lie on. It wasn't enough to make a soft bed, but it covered the rocky floor and dampened the chill.

"Are you sure you have enough food for a couple of days?" I asked Hennie as I prepared to set off the next morning.

"Probably not, but we will find more when we need it. Tey, don't worry. You won't be gone that long."

"If I cannot find a village within a day's walk, I will come back. So I will be gone no more than two full days."

"We will be fine."

She showed me the dagger strapped to her forearm in one of

my wrist sheaths. A single dagger would do little to dissuade anyone who found them, especially since it would be apparent Hennie didn't know what to do with it, but that was all I could do. It had to be me who went for supplies, and I couldn't stay here to protect them at the same time. I couldn't take them with me either, not with the cut on Seti's foot still healing.

Hennie had quietly said it would be good for Seti and me to have some time apart. She didn't mention her knees, but I noticed the way she hobbled. Walking on the sand seemed to have irritated her bad knees. Time to rest would be good for Hennie, too.

Eventually, I set off, although not without several backward glances. Once the cave was out of sight, it was easier to turn my mind to my task. Find a village. Trade for supplies. I had selected a couple of items from the little bag Intef gave me as we left the palace. Amongst the jewellery studded with expensive gems, I found several plain finger rings, much like my mother's. These were less valuable and would be easier to trade. I had chosen three — a plain gold band, a plain silver one, and a silver that had just the tiniest flecks of lapis lazuli. I had no idea how much they were worth, although the gold would be the lesser, since silver was more highly prized.

I ran through my mental list of the supplies we needed, calculating different combinations and figuring how I might carry enough. Of course, it would all be for nothing if I didn't reach a village today. I would find somewhere to camp tonight and head back to the cave in the morning. Or perhaps I would just turn back and walk through the night. If I had to sleep, I'd rather do it at the cave, where at least I could protect them if necessary.

As I walked, I watched for better places to live. The cave Nef found was good enough, but more varied food and a bigger stream would make other locations worth considering. I had only been walking for a couple of hours before I spotted smoke. Heartened, I walked a little faster. The sun was an hour or so past its peak as the village came into sight. If I could get supplies quickly, I could be back at the cave tonight. I'd be walking the last couple of hours in the dark, but it would be worth it.

It didn't take long to find the market. It was only a small village, and the market reflected that, but I was able to get everything we needed. An hour later, weighed down with various packs and baskets, and minus two of the finger rings, I set off again.

Now that I didn't have to worry about lists of supplies, I could turn my mind to other practicalities, like what to do if someone found us. It might not be possible to identify whether they were actually searching for us or merely had the misfortune to stumble over us. Given we had already escaped our pursuers twice, perhaps they would try a different tactic. They might send untrained men. Men who pretended to be nothing more than goat herders or farmers, and who could report our location before I ever realised what they were.

So if someone found us, and there was only one person, or maybe two, I would kill them. I couldn't risk doing anything else. But if it was more than two men, we would have to slip away. I wasn't sure how many I could take on myself. Two I was pretty confident about, especially if they were untrained. But if they sent an entire squad after us? Or even another half squad? No one person could take on that many men alone, no matter how skilled they were, and I couldn't risk being killed or injured myself. I couldn't protect the girls — or Hennie — if I was dead.

So if more than two men found us, we would leave if we could. We would walk along the coastline until we found a wharf. Then we would get on the first ship we could and go wherever it took us. We would make a new life for ourselves somewhere far away from Egypt. Surely then we would be safe.

TWENTY

TEY

It was well past sunset before I approached our cave. To my alarm, a fire burned at the entrance, giving a clear signal to anyone in the area that someone was there. But when I got closer, I spotted the figure sitting beside it.

"Hennie," I called softly, not wanting to startle her. "It is me."

"Tey." She got to her feet rather stiffly. It seemed her knees were still painful. "I did not expect to see you tonight."

"There is a village not much more than a half day's walk," I said.

"You could have stayed the night there. You must have walked a very long way today."

"I didn't want to leave you alone overnight if I didn't have to."

"We would have been fine. I was going to keep watch."

"All night?"

"It is no more than you have done yourself many times."

Hennie's tone was defensive and I shut my mouth before I reminded her I was trained for such things. Perhaps I didn't give her enough opportunity to feel like she contributed. I had thought I shouldn't expect too much of such an old woman — she must be well into her forties, although I had never asked — but perhaps she could do more than I realised. Maybe I had been doing too much for all of them.

The girls must have heard me, for they came out, yawning and blinking in the light from the fire. All three crowded around to rummage through the packs and see what I brought. The first thing Hennie found was the little blue jar I had set at the top of one pack. She removed the stopper and sniffed the contents.

"Hmm, smells like sage," she said. "I don't suppose this is arnica?"

"I thought it might help your knees," I said. "And Seti's foot."

"Oh, thank you, dear."

Hennie pulled up her tunic and rubbed the cream on her knees. They must have been more painful than she let on.

Nef found the clay jar of honey and stuck her finger in. I had planned to hide that away and bring it out as a treat. As Nef licked her finger, Seti tried to snatch the jar from her. It landed on the ground, smashing against the rocks.

"That was your fault." Nef glared at Seti even as she licked the last of the honey off her finger.

"I didn't get any," Seti wailed.

She crouched beside the broken jar and scooped up some of the honey.

I turned away so they wouldn't see me roll my eyes. Of course, Seti would ruin the one treat I brought.

"Now girls, don't fight." Hennie intervened before I snapped at them. "Seti, don't eat that. It will have little shards of the broken jar through it. Why don't you go find me a handful of leaves I can scrape it up with?"

"It is ruined," Seti said with a sob. "It isn't fair."

"It wouldn't have gotten broken if you hadn't snatched it," Nef said with a glare.

"Is there more?" Seti turned a hopeful look on me.

"There were more important things to bring than jars of honey," I said curtly.

"You should have brought more," she said.

I took a deep breath and tried to swallow my angry response.

"Seti, leaves," Hennie said. "Nef, you can go help her."

"But it is Seti's fault the jar got broken," Nef said. "I didn't do anything."

"If you weren't trying to stop her from taking the honey, it wouldn't have happened. You are both responsible and you can both go find something I can use to clean up this mess."

"Or they could clean it themselves," I muttered.

Hennie shot me a look.

"And they would likely cut themselves and then we would have bleeding fingers to deal with on top of everything else," she said.

Her tone was sharper than usual and I realised with a pang she was annoyed with me. But why? Because I wanted the girls to learn how to do things for themselves? Because I didn't like to see Hennie acting as their servant?

Maybe it is because you are too impatient with them, a little voice inside me whispered. You should think before you speak, especially when it comes to Seti.

I carried the packs into the cave and stacked them against the wall. I would talk to Hennie tomorrow and smooth things over with her. I was too tired not to make a mess of it tonight.

"Go get some sleep, Tey," Hennie said. "I will sit up."

I nodded, suddenly too weary to even reply. I wrapped myself in one of the new blankets and was asleep almost as soon as I lay down.

Over the next few days, we settled into our new home. The blankets and other supplies I brought from the village made life easier, although we encountered challenges every day. The girls went to check the rock pools after each high tide, but sometimes came back empty-handed. At least we had oysters and the little crabs. But their population dwindled much sooner than I expected and we had to go further down the beach each day in search of food. We had found only two sea bird nests nearby and once we had taken a couple of eggs from each, I left them alone.

Taking all their eggs would mean no baby birds and no more eggs in future seasons. I tried hunting, but the surrounding vegetation didn't seem to hold anything I could chase down with a dagger.

We rationed the supplies, but not even two weeks had passed before we needed more. I emptied the bag of gems and found only one more plain gold finger ring. Once I had used that, I would need to take the ones with the gems. They were far more valuable and conspicuous. I wouldn't get a fair trade for them either, not for goods I could carry by myself.

"Something on your mind?" Hennie asked me later that day.

I had been turning over the ground for an expansion to our new vegetable garden and it was only when she spoke that I realised I had stopped digging and was instead scowling at the sea. I tried to find a reply that would be honest enough without worrying her.

"I have seen you checking the supplies," Hennie said. "Twice yesterday and then again today. You are worried."

"We are going through them so fast. I thought they would last at least a month."

"The girls are growing," Hennie said. "They are eating more."

"It seems like they are eating twice what they were a few weeks ago."

"Perhaps this is not the best place for us to settle. Maybe we should find somewhere closer to the village. Or even in the village. I don't understand why you think we need to be so far away from anyone else."

"To make us harder to find," I said. "They already found us in Nubet. Once you disappeared, it would be logical to assume you went with us, so now they know the girls are with two women. We stand out even more now to anyone who hears a description of the four of us."

Hennie was silent for a few moments.

"I am sorry," she said at last. "I didn't realise my coming with you would cause so much trouble."

"No, Hennie, I didn't mean it like that. I don't know what I would do without you. I was just trying to explain why we need to stay out of sight. If people see me coming and going, I am just one woman alone and that doesn't raise much suspicion. I don't want anyone to see you and the girls. Besides, being closer to a village won't help. We don't have much left to trade for supplies. I may have to leave you for a while and try to get some work."

"Tey, no. We need to stay together. I couldn't protect the girls if someone found us while you were gone."

"It could just as easily happen if I am gone for the day as if I am gone for a week or two."

"No, it is out of the question. We must stay together."

Hennie so rarely insisted on anything that I couldn't argue with her about this.

"I will figure something out," I said.

"We will figure it out together, Tey dear. You do not have to do this alone. We can all help, even the girls."

"They are too young to understand."

"I think they understand more than you give them credit for. Most children don't endure being smuggled away from their home and everyone they love and hidden away to protect them from assassins. They have had to grow up much faster than other children their age. Perhaps you could try letting them in when you make our plans. Let them help. It would be good for them — both of them — to know you trust them."

"I cannot trust them," I said. "They knew they were not supposed to tell anyone who they were, but Seti told you the first chance she got."

"She was what, seven years old? A mere child. Seti is doing her best, but children sometimes forget. She must be nine now and Nef would be ten or eleven. Give them a chance and they might surprise you."

I pursed my lips and merely shook my head. I didn't want to argue with Hennie, but I knew to my core I couldn't trust Seti.

TWENTY-ONE
SETI

I spent all morning planning what I would say to Tey. She wouldn't like what I wanted to ask, but I was sure she would say yes if I could get my words right. I even waited for the best moment to talk to her, when she wasn't busy working on the vegetable garden and she wasn't frowning. When she went walking off down the beach, I saw my chance.

"Tey." I ran to catch up with her. "Can I talk to you?"

"What is it, Seti?"

She shaded her eyes as she looked out at the water. Was it a good or bad sign she didn't look at me? It might mean she was thinking about something, in which case she might just say no because she was too busy to think about anything else. Or it might mean she was mad at me again. I thought hard about what I might have done to make her mad today, but couldn't think of anything. I took a deep breath and said it.

"Tey, I want to practice. Just in a very small way," I rushed on. "So next time I can do more. I helped last time. Really helped. But I could do much better if I practiced."

"What are you talking about?"

Tey looked at me, only for a moment, then she shook her head and kept walking. I hurried after her.

"With the bad thing," I said. "I need to learn how to make it help me."

She whirled around and loomed over me.

"No, Seti. Promise me you will not try to use your ability again."

I took a step back, sinking down to my ankles in the soft sand.

"But there is nobody to see me out here," I said. "We wouldn't have escaped if it wasn't for me. If I didn't let the bad thing out, they would have caught us."

"That took so much out of you, you were unconscious for hours afterwards," she said. "You could kill yourself next time. You are not to use your ability again."

"You said we would find someone who could teach me," I said. "I know the Sand Wanderers didn't have anyone who could, but I thought now we are near a village…"

"When I said that, I didn't know how using your ability could affect you. We are not discussing this, Seti. It is too dangerous and you could kill yourself."

She strode off, making her shoulders hunched over in the way she did when she didn't want to talk to anyone. A tear fell out of my eye as I watched her go. She wouldn't even talk with me. I knew I could convince her if we could just talk about it.

TWENTY-TWO

TEY

My pulse drummed in my ears as I strode away from Seti. I thought maybe she called after me again, but between my pounding heart and the roar of the waves, I couldn't hear what she said. I tucked my head down and kept going. She would assume I hadn't heard her.

For a while, I walked, or rather stomped, along the beach, kicking up the sand with each step. I was so angry I couldn't even think. But gradually the rushing of the waves, the cries of the sea birds, and the solitude of the empty beach calmed me.

What in Aten's name was Seti thinking? She had no control over the bad thing, as she called it, and we had no way of knowing how powerful it was. Until she used her ability in the desert, I hadn't realised it took something from her. Used something within her, although whether it was energy or her essential essence or something else, I didn't know. We couldn't afford for her to experiment. What if whatever got used up couldn't be replenished? What if she could only use her ability so much before it killed her? We didn't know enough about it to risk her using it again.

We might not have escaped without her ability. Our pursuers were close — too close — and her storm delayed them long enough for us to hide. No, I would have thought of something. I always did. Surely, I would have kept them safe even without Seti's ability. But a little voice inside me said that maybe I wasn't enough on my own. Maybe I needed help to keep them safe.

I walked a long way before I felt calm enough to turn back. Hennie said I needed to try harder with Seti, but that girl provoked me in a way I had never experienced before. It seemed like the worst kind of joke that the big adventure I had spent my life training for turned out to be mothering two pampered princesses.

"I will go to the village tomorrow," I told Hennie and the girls as we ate our evening meal. "I will leave before dawn, so if there is anything you want, tell me tonight."

"Can you get some more honey?" Seti asked. "You didn't bring back enough last time."

Irritation flared within me. The only reason there wasn't enough was because Seti broke the jar. I exhaled, trying to calm myself before I replied.

"Onions," Hennie said quickly. "Fruit. I think we have eaten all the ripe dates within an easy walk. And I used the last of the emmer yesterday."

I nodded, thankful she had saved me from needing to respond to Seti.

"Nef, anything you would like?" I asked.

"Some cheese?" she suggested. "And maybe some melon juice."

"Melon juice would be too heavy," I said. "Sorry, but I would have to leave other things behind to manage it."

"Just cheese then," Nef said. "I am dying for some cheese."

I swallowed my last oyster and got to my feet.

"You didn't ask what I wanted," Seti said.

"You already asked for honey."

"But you asked Nef if she wanted anything. You didn't ask me."

What in Aten's name did she want from me? Could she not

understand she'd already had her turn to make a request? Why would I ask her what she wanted after she had already told me? I swallowed the irritable reply that threatened to burst out of me and walked away.

I woke well before dawn the next morning. Hennie and the girls didn't even stir as I left the cave. How fortunate for them to sleep as late as they wanted while I was up early to walk all day to fetch supplies for them. Maybe next time I would take Nef with me. Hennie kept saying the girls needed more responsibility. Well, Nef could see what it was like to travel so far and only be able to bring back what you could carry yourself.

The weather echoed my mood today with a grey sky and fog hanging over the water. I almost turned back, thinking I would wait a day or two until the weather cleared. It would be a miserable journey if I had to do it in the rain and there was nothing we needed so badly that it couldn't wait a couple of days. But if I went back, I'd have to face the girls' disappointment that I had returned without the items they requested, and I wasn't sure I could trust myself not to snap back. A day apart would be good for all of us.

The sky cleared as I walked and by the time I reached the village, there was no sign of rain. I chose supplies carefully, mindful of how much I could carry. Onions, emmer, dates and cheese as requested by Hennie and Nef. Lettuce, cucumber, beans, radishes and lentils. A needle and thread, as we had nothing with which to mend our clothes and Seti had a tear through one sleeve. Extra blankets. A second cooking pot. Hennie had said nothing about managing with only one, but a second would be useful and I could carry the vegetables back in it, anyway. I hesitated over the jars of honey, my hand lingering on the smallest, but my mouth watered when I saw some pomegranates. That was something I hadn't tasted in a long time.

I took two pomegranates and set my packages down while I ate one. It was sweet and juicy, and I was tempted to eat the other straight away. I tucked it away in a pack, telling myself I would take it back for Hennie, but knowing I would probably eat it on the way. As I picked up my packages, someone spoke from behind me.

"Hello there."

A male voice, and not an old one.

I turned and found myself looking into a pair of dark brown eyes. He was slightly taller than me, with the sun-browned skin of a farmer. He wore a *shendyt* and no shirt, as was usual for most men, and my gaze swept over his chest before I could stop myself. My cheeks heated and I turned away, fussing with my packs.

"You will not say hello back?" he asked. "It is tough enough to get up the courage to speak to a pretty girl, but it is a million times worse when she won't reply."

I turned back to him, but my thoughts whirled and I felt so flustered that I couldn't find anything to say. He waited, his lips twitching as if he wanted to smile at me, but restrained himself. Feeling like an idiot that I hadn't managed to say even hello, I picked up my last pack and hurried away.

TWENTY-THREE
TEY

As I rushed through the market, I didn't know what to think. I had never experienced that sort of reaction to a boy before. He's not a boy, a little voice inside me whispered. He's a man. I stopped on the edge of the market to adjust a pack digging into my shoulder. Still absorbed in my thoughts, I didn't notice the two women nearby at first.

"She is reputed to be very accurate," one said.

"I don't know," the other replied. "How could she even have that sort of information?"

"From the gods, of course. I think you should go. The oracle might give you the information you need. At least if she says you will never bear a child, then you know and you can stop trying."

"I don't think I would want to hear it," the second woman said. "Even if it is the truth. Let me keep on hoping."

"It is destroying you. I see it, month after month. You are devastated every time."

"And think how much more devastated I will be if I learn it has all been for nothing. That I will never have a child, no matter how much I want one."

"There are other ways of getting children if you cannot bear one yourself. You know Iset, don't you? She lives right on the edge of the village in that tiny cottage that always looks like it is about to fall down."

"I have never spoken to her, but I know who you mean."

"I heard she is with child again. They cannot afford to feed the children they have. If you knew you would never bear your own, you could offer to take one of hers and raise it. And if you don't want one of her babes, or she won't give one up, I can think of at least three other women with more children than they can feed. Surely one of them would be pleased to ease their burden if you offered."

"I don't want someone else's child and I don't want to hear the oracle tell me I will never have my own."

"Just think about it, yes? Promise me that much."

Before I could talk myself out of it, I approached them.

"Excuse me," I said. "I couldn't help overhearing you. Is there an oracle nearby?"

"She lives in a cave about a day's walk north of here," said the woman who had been trying to persuade her friend. She pointed. "That way."

"If I wanted to talk to her, what would I need to do?" I asked.

"You go and she decides whether she will speak with you. She doesn't talk to everyone. To some, she says she has nothing for them and sends them away. But others, she will speak with and give them such wisdom as she has."

"How would I find her? Is there a landmark that would tell me I am near her cave?"

"As you walk along the shoreline, you will come to a spot where the shore curves like a writhing snake. There is a large rock on the beach in the central curve. Turn inland there and walk west for about half a league. Her cave is near a large fig tree, which has been cleaved in two by lightning. It is another half day's walk to the next town if you miss the place to turn. If you find yourself at the wharf, you have gone too far. If you go, make sure you take something for her. She will expect payment if she speaks to you."

I had much to think about as I made my way back to our cave.

Should we go to the oracle? She might know whether our pursuers would catch up to us or whether I could do anything else to keep the girls safe. I could go alone, but what if it was not me the oracle had information for? She might want to talk to one of the girls, or even Hennie. It would be best if we all went together. We finally had an opportunity to get some information. Maybe it would mean we didn't have to keep living in constant fear of being found.

With that decision out of the way, I turned my thoughts to the man I met. My cheeks heated again at the realisation he must have seen me looking at his chest. I had never experienced the childish crushes I heard other girls talking about. The boys I knew growing up all seemed silly and immature, and they didn't hold my interest enough to divert me from my training. But this man, he was different. I felt... something. An attraction to him. I wanted to know who he was.

I pushed the thoughts away. There was no time for men. I had enough to manage with looking after Hennie and the girls. There was no time for romance or any such nonsense.

TWENTY-FOUR

TEY

The girls were waiting on the beach when I returned.

"Tey," Nef called and waved.

Seti waved too, an exuberant two-armed wave that told me she was trying to be extra nice. Probably because she was expecting honey. It was only then I remembered I didn't get any. I had been intending to, but got distracted by the pomegranates and then the man.

There were tears when Seti learned there was no honey and she stomped off down the beach. Nef slipped away after her.

"Tey," Hennie said quietly. "Go on."

"What?"

"Go after her. You two should talk."

"About what?"

Hennie shook her head.

"Tey, the two of you cannot go on like this. The tension affects all of us, not just you and Seti."

"I didn't not bring honey just to be mean. I forgot."

"She is a child, Tey, and you are the closest thing she has to a mother. I know you find her trying, but you are the adult and it is up to you to mend your relationship."

"I gave up everything for those girls." My tone was bitter. "They don't appreciate it in the slightest."

"They are too young to understand what you have done. They will one day, when they are older. Besides, you didn't do it for them. From what you have told me, you did it for yourself."

I stared at her.

"How can you say such a thing? I gave up my home, my family, my life to take them away. What do I get out of this? Nothing. Not payment, not gratitude, not... anything."

Hennie sighed and shook her head.

"Just think about it, dear. Think about why you really did it. I am not saying it wasn't noble and necessary and wonderful, only that I don't think you did it for the reasons you tell yourself."

I resisted the urge to stomp away like Seti. I didn't realise Nef had come back until she spoke.

"Tey, we do appreciate what you did," she said.

"I didn't mean for you to hear that." My cheeks heated with shame. I wouldn't have said most of that if I realised Nef was there.

"We would much rather be with you than with some man soldier," she said. "I think we would always be afraid of him, but you make us feel safe. But I hate the way you and Seti argue, and then she goes off crying. She always expects me to side with her since we are sisters, but I feel like I have to side with you since you keep us safe and you saved me when the bad men got me, but then she gets mad at me and we fight and I hate it."

She finished in a rush and burst into tears.

My whole body felt hot with embarrassment and all I wanted to do was get away.

"I am going for a walk," I said, getting to my feet.

"Perhaps you could find Seti on your way back," Hennie said.

I didn't reply.

I walked along the beach, letting the breeze and the rush of the waves soothe me. I had been so wrapped up in how I felt that I hadn't noticed the impact it was having on everyone else. This was my family now, whether I liked it or not. I needed to stop wishing Seti was a different person. Surely after living with her for more than two years, I should be used to her by now, but I only found her more frustrating as time passed. Papa would be ashamed if he knew how I had let my emotions and my temper influence me. I held up my hand to look at my mother's ring. It caught the moonlight and glinted, as if conveying a message from her.

"I wish you were here to tell me what to do, Mama," I whispered. "I hardly remember you anymore and I am afraid I will forget you entirely."

If I had hoped to receive some mystic message from my mother, or at least a sense of comfort, I was disappointed. I was almost back at the cave when I spotted Seti. She perched on a rock, her knees drawn up to her chest. I hesitated. She hadn't seen me yet, so I could keep walking. We didn't have to talk tonight. But then she turned her head and the stiffening of her shoulders told me she had spotted me.

Seti didn't look up as I sat beside her. I looked out at the sea, its waves restless even so late. The moon was still low and the water sparkled as it moved beneath it.

"It is so beautiful here," I said.

I couldn't think of anything else to say. Didn't know how to start the conversation I knew we had to have.

"It is." Seti sniffled, but it didn't sound like the fake sniff she used when she wanted attention.

"Are you cold?" I asked.

"A little."

"Come here."

I put my arm around her shoulders, surprised to realise this might be the first time I had hugged her.

She stiffened, and I thought she would pull away, but then she leaned against me. After a moment, she rested her head on my shoulder and sniffled again.

"Seti." I still didn't know what to say.

"Do you hate me because of the bad thing?" she asked.

"What? Of course not."

"If I didn't have the bad thing, would you hate me less?"

"Seti, I don't hate you."

"You do," she said. "Sometimes anyway."

I sighed. She was right, and lying about it wouldn't mend our relationship. I was ashamed to realise I had never thought about how my reactions to her must make her feel. I had been too consumed with my own feelings.

"I find you... frustrating," I said. "There is something about you that... I don't know how to explain it."

"It is because we are so much alike. That is what Grandmother says, anyway."

Hennie had said the same thing to me, but I hadn't understood what she meant.

"You talk to Hennie about me?" I asked.

I felt her shrug.

"When we fight, she sometimes comes and finds me. She tries to make me feel better."

"Seti, I am sorry. I never wanted children and I don't know how to be your mother."

"I wish you did, though," she said quietly. "I don't remember my mother."

"Me either. Mine went to the West when I was very young. I wasn't much older than you were."

"I didn't know that." She raised her head to look at me. "I thought you left her and your father to take us away."

"I left my father, and I miss him terribly. I even miss my little brother."

"The one who is our sister's captain."

"Yes, Intef."

"I was a bit scared of him."

"He would never hurt you."

He might, though, if it was the only way to protect his beloved queen. Perhaps when he was making arrangements to send the girls away, it was as much to save himself from killing them as to save their lives.

"I miss our little brother," Seti said. "Sort of. We never saw him much."

"Why not?"

"He was always sick. They didn't let us spend much time with him so it wouldn't hurt when he went to the West."

"He still lives," I said. "I haven't had a chance to tell you yet, but the men who found us when we were with the Sand Wanderers said he was Pharaoh. He calls himself Tutankhamun now."

She was quiet for a while, digesting this.

"Is our sister still queen?" she asked.

"Yes, she is now called Ankhesenamun."

"Ankhesenamun. I like it."

"Your brother and sister's new names honour Amun. I think that's one of the old gods. I suppose that means your father's rule about only worshipping Aten has been revoked. "

"I have never heard of Amun," she said. "Do you think that means I could worship a different god if I wanted to?"

"I suppose so. If Pharaoh and his queen worship an old god, I guess we can worship whoever we want."

She was silent for a few moments.

"Tey, do you ever wonder whether the gods really exist?" she asked.

Her question took me by surprise and it took me a few moments to find a response.

"I don't think I have ever thought about it," I said.

After all, every time I saw the sun or felt its rays on my skin, I knew that was Aten. How could I doubt his existence when I saw evidence of him every day? But what about all the other gods? How did we know they existed?

"Do you have doubts?" I asked, rather awkwardly. I was not equipped for a conversation like this.

I felt her shrug against me.

"I don't know," she said. "Maybe."

We were silent for a while after that. I looked out at the moon and the sparkling water and thought about whether Aten existed even at night when I couldn't see him. We should definitely all go to the oracle. Perhaps it would be Seti she had wisdom for, some-thing that might help her with these big questions I hadn't realised she was grappling with.

"I know what it is like to wonder about your loved ones." I was on surer ground with this topic. Nobody had ever asked how I knew Papa or Intef existed. "I will never know when my father goes to the West. I won't know if my brother ever marries or if he has children."

He would never marry, though. No woman could ever take Ankhesenamun's place in his heart.

"This is a horrible kind of life," Seti said, with something that might have been a sob. "I wish we could go home. Not because we lived in a palace and had servants and everything. But because we would be with our sister and our brother. I would rather go home and if the bad men find me and kill me, well…"

Her voice trailed away.

I understood. How many times had I thought it would be better to take them back to Akhetaten and let the situation resolve itself one way or another? Wouldn't that be better than a life spent on the run? Always looking over our shoulders, always wondering when they would next catch up to us? We needed relief from the constant watching and waiting. We needed whatever the oracle could tell us. All this time I had been thinking only about how tired I was of living like this. I hadn't stopped to think about how the others must feel.

"I know we cannot," she said before I could think of a reply. "I just wish we could."

"I know."

We were silent for a while after that. I didn't realise I was crying until the breeze dried the tears on my cheeks.

"Seti, I am sorry," I said. "I expected this to be much easier than it is. I never thought about what you and Nef were going through. I think I forgot you are human, and children at that."

"Nef tries to be grown up, but I cannot. I don't feel at all grown up."

"You are not and you don't have to pretend to be."

"Tey, if I ask you something, will you promise you won't get mad at me?"

I knew what she wanted to ask. I took a deep breath and told myself I would really listen.

"Go on," I said.

"I need to learn how to make the bad thing listen to me. It helped us get away from the bad men, but it took too much of me with it and that made me fall asleep. If I could learn about it while we are here, where there is nobody else around to see, I might do better next time."

"I don't know, Seti. I fear you won't be able to control it. That the next time you use it might be the time it takes more than you can give."

"It could help us. It might save us again one day, but if I don't know how to use it… maybe that is how it kills me."

I could see the logic in her argument, but I couldn't forget the way she looked when she collapsed in the desert.

"Why do you call it the bad thing?" I asked.

"Because it shouldn't be there. Because there is something wrong with me that I have this thing inside me."

"Seti, there is nothing wrong with you. It is just… a part of you. A gift."

"From who?"

"The gods, I suppose."

"Aten?"

"Maybe, or one of the old gods."

"Amun?"

"I don't know, Seti. I know little about the old gods." But something teased at my memory. A half-remembered tale about a lion goddess who drank a river of blood and wanted to destroy the world. "Sekhmet, maybe. The goddess of chaos."

"I have never heard of her."

"No, I suppose you wouldn't have."

It was her father, after all, who outlawed the old gods and allowed only his favourite to be worshipped.

"You think Sekhmet put the bad thing inside me?"

"Maybe. Her or one of the other gods."

"I want to be alone." Seti shook off my arm and rose. She ran off.

I let her go. I hadn't realised how much her "bad thing" distressed her. That it might be a gift from the gods was clearly a new thought for her. She needed time to process it. Then we could talk again.

TWENTY-FIVE

SETI

All this time I thought Tey hated me because of the bad thing and because she had to leave her family to look after me and Nef. But she thought the bad thing might be from the gods. So maybe that meant she didn't think it was a bad thing after all.

"Is it true?" I whispered to the bad thing. "Did the goddess Sekhmet put you inside me?"

The bad thing didn't answer. I couldn't even feel it at the moment. It wasn't rumbling around in my belly like it did when it wanted to come out. Maybe it was asleep.

"What should I call you then?" I asked it. "If a goddess put you in me, I don't think I should call you the bad thing anymore."

I walked along the beach, only a little way so Tey wouldn't get mad at me for going off by myself. The waves rolled in and out. They were pretty the way they shimmered in the moonlight. They weren't as pretty during the day, even though they sparkled in the sunlight too. The water rushed in over my toes. It was too cold, but when the waves came back, I let them go over my feet again.

Maybe the bad thing was Sekhmet. Did I have a goddess living inside my belly? I thought about this for a good long while, but decided the bad thing couldn't be a goddess. She would get all wet and messy every time I ate and surely a goddess wouldn't want to live like that. So I didn't have Sekhmet inside my belly, but maybe she had put something there.

Maybe the bad thing had feelings. It might be sad I kept calling it the bad thing. Maybe it didn't like living inside me and when it got angry and flew up my throat and out of my mouth, it was trying to get away from me. But it couldn't leave me for long and once it wasn't angry anymore, it had to go back down inside my belly.

I should try to be nicer to the bad thing. I only ever talked to it when I was angry, but maybe if I talked to it when I was feeling nice, it wouldn't get so mad.

Was Tey thinking about whether she should be nicer to me? She wasn't always as mean as she used to be, but she still got mean sometimes, like when the honey jar broke. Grandmother said she wasn't *trying* to be mean, but that Tey got upset because I was just as stubborn as her and neither one of us ever wanted to give in.

One of our tutors told us a story once. He called it a fable and it had a bunch of animals who learned about being nice to each other and then they all became friends. There was a crocodile and a duck and a bug, but I couldn't remember what happened to them. I wish I did. It might be useful now.

TWENTY-SIX

TEY

Seti kept to herself that evening and didn't even come to eat with us. I spotted her sitting on the rocks by the shoreline, silhouetted against the night sky.

"What happened between the two of you?" Hennie asked.

"We talked. We didn't fight," I added quickly, "as I am sure you are thinking. I guess some of it was things she hadn't considered before. She needs time to think."

"I will take her some food," Hennie said.

She sat with Seti for a while, and when she returned, she seemed preoccupied.

"Is she well?" I asked.

"Hmm? Oh, yes, well enough. Like you said, she needs to think."

I wondered how much of our conversation Seti had told her and what of it Hennie thought she needed to think about.

Seti slipped back into the cave just before bed. She wrapped herself in a blanket and lay on her bed mat without saying a word. By morning, she seemed more or less back to her usual self, if a little subdued.

"I forgot to tell you last night," I said to Hennie as we broke our fast with a loaf of fresh bread she had risen early to cook over the fire. Both girls had taken their share down to the beach. "There is an oracle, only a day or so further than the village."

"Oracles are temperamental," Hennie said. "We might go all that way and find she has nothing to say to us."

"That is a possibility. The woman who told me about her said she refuses to speak to some people. But what is the risk? We spend a couple of days walking for nothing. It is not like we have other things we need to do more urgently."

"A couple of days' walking might be nothing to you, but it will be painful for me."

It wasn't like Hennie to complain about her knees.

"I could take the girls while you stay here."

"Maybe you should go alone. You will travel faster by yourself, anyway."

Not all that long ago, Hennie was convinced we had to stay together. What had made her change her mind?

"But what if it is not me the oracle has wisdom for? It might be one of the girls she wants to speak with. Seti, perhaps. The oracle might tell her how to harness her ability, or at least how she might learn such a thing. Seti keeps asking to practice and I would feel much easier about it if we could find someone to teach her safely. If I go alone and learn nothing, I would have to come back and take the girls to her. Otherwise, we will never know whether she might have had information that would benefit us."

"But what are you hoping the oracle might tell you?" Hennie asked.

"About our pursuers. Whether they will find us again. Maybe even when. If we knew they wouldn't, we could stop looking behind us."

"From what I have heard, an oracle's wisdom is not usually that specific. Would you still think it worth the journey if you knew that all she could tell us is that they *will* find us again, but not when or how?"

"Then at least we would know that much. It is the uncertainty I hate. The waiting and wondering and praying they aren't just behind us while never knowing whether maybe they have finally given up."

Hennie gave a great sigh.

"I am so tired of living in fear, Tey," she said. "Maybe we should leave Egypt. You have talked before about going to another country. Perhaps we could find somewhere where women who want to forge their own path are not considered so strange as they are here."

"There is a place. Sparta. My father spoke of it once. They train both men and women to be soldiers."

"There, that is exactly what we need. We could blend in, and if everyone is trained the way you are, we would be safer there."

"What if the queen were to die?" Why hadn't I thought of this before? "Their sister. If she died, Nef would be next in line for the throne. Do we have the right to take her away to somewhere she might never be found given the possibility she might be queen one day?"

"Their sister has surely birthed a child by now, likely a girl," Hennie said. "After all, their mother had many girls. Wouldn't the queen's daughter be higher in the line of succession than her sister?"

"I don't know. I only know there is a possibility that Nef could be queen."

"It has never bothered you before."

"I knew she was next in line for the throne, but my focus has always been on keeping the girls safe," I said. "I never thought about what it would mean for Nef if their sister were to die."

"There are many dangers facing a queen, but our responsibility is to Nef and Seti, not their sister. We have no obligation to keep the girls here in case the queen dies."

"I wasn't thinking about an obligation to their sister. Imagine the life Nef would lead if she was queen."

"But if they come for her, we won't know why. Even if they said they had come because her sister was dead, how would we know whether that was the truth?"

"I would kill anyone who got that close," I said.

"And that might be the messenger who came to summon her back."

"They wouldn't send soldiers with a message like that. It would be an official. Someone very high ranking."

"Perhaps they would send your brother? If he came, you would trust him, would you not?"

"As long as he is alive, the queen is too, and he wouldn't leave her long enough for such a journey."

"You still assume she will die on an assassin's dagger. There are other dangers a woman faces. Childbirth, injury, disease. Things your brother cannot prevent, no matter how skilled he is."

I laughed.

"You don't know my brother," I said. "He is very determined and he loves her more than life itself. I doubt there is anything that could befall her that he wouldn't fight. Even if she went to the underworld, he would find a way to follow her there."

"Tell me, Tey. How is it that your brother knows the queen so intimately? How does the son of a foot soldier become the queen's captain?"

"They met as children. He was seven years old, I think, or thereabouts, and he decided he loved her the day they met. I remember him telling our father that evening. Papa told him not to waste his life loving a woman he could never have and Intef was adamant his feelings would never change. He told Papa he would be her captain one day. I guess he thought it was the only way a commoner could be close to her. He has trained for that ever since."

"Just as you prepared for your own big adventure," Hennie said. "It sounds like your father raised two very strong-willed children."

"He did, and I think we caused him no small amount of grief."

"I doubt that, Tey. Knowing you as I do, I am certain your father is extremely proud. He would worry about you, his only daughter, gone so far away and doing Aten-only-knows what, but

I cannot imagine that a man who raises a daughter like you could be anything other than very, very proud of her."

Tears welled, sudden and unexpected. I dashed them away. Hennie looked out at the water and kindly pretended not to notice.

TWENTY-SEVEN

TEY

It took most of the day to convince Hennie we should go to the oracle, but eventually we decided to leave the following morning. She frowned as we packed our supplies.

"You could stay here," I said again, assuming she was still unhappy with our decision. "It is only three days."

"We will take supplies for four days," Hennie said. "We might have to wait if others arrive before us."

"I can manage with the girls by myself, and I promise I will not kill Seti."

If I had thought she might laugh at that, I was wrong. She only frowned at our growing pile of packs.

"Or perhaps we will arrive on a day she has decided not to see anyone," she said. "We might have to wait a day or two, so supplies for six days."

"The walk will be too much for you. Remember how much your knees hurt by the time we got here?"

"If one of the girls falls ill or is injured, we will have to stop somewhere along the way. Perhaps supplies for eight days."

"Hennie, stop." I placed my hand on her arm. "What is the matter?"

"I just want to be prepared. As you said, we have little that is of small enough value to trade for supplies. We will have to make do with whatever we take from here."

"It is unlike you to fuss so much."

Hennie sighed.

"I am still not convinced we should do this. I don't see how anything good can come of it."

"But what about what we might learn?"

"That is what I am afraid of. I know you think this will give you peace of mind, but what if it only makes things worse?"

"Hennie, I think you should stay here. Have some time to yourself without needing to look after anyone else. We will be back before you even miss us."

"No. If you take the girls, I am coming too. I will only spend the time worrying otherwise. And what if something happens along the way? What if someone catches up to you and you have to flee with the girls? There might not be time to come back for me, and I will be here, waiting, wondering every day whether today is the day you will return."

"Nothing will happen to us," I said. "And I promise you, we will come back. Even if someone finds us and we need to flee, I will come back for you. I would never disappear with the girls and leave you wondering."

"You might have no choice. And I would understand. Truly, I would. But I cannot bear the thought of it and I will not stay behind alone."

There was no point trying to persuade her otherwise. We were silent as we finished packing.

We set off after breakfast the following morning. By noon, the girls had grown tired and lagged behind. They were stronger than they once were, but I had underestimated their ability to cope with walking for an entire day. Even Hennie moved too slowly, although she tried hard to keep up and she never once mentioned her bad knees.

Seti complained the most. About everything. Her feet hurt. Her legs were tired. The wind blew in the wrong direction and she kept getting hair in her eyes. She had sand in her sandals and she was hungry and thirsty. She went on and on until I wondered whether we had anything I might tie around her mouth to keep her quiet for a while. At least Nef was mostly silent, although she walked no faster than Seti.

It was midafternoon before we reached the village. We should have been here a couple of hours ago. The oracle was another full day's walk away, or maybe closer to two at the pace we were moving. Hennie had been right to bring extra supplies.

We had nothing to trade for a night's accommodation so we camped on the beach. Seti complained bitterly about that, even though we had brought blankets. There were no rocky pools like near our cave and although I walked along the shoreline for a while, I didn't spot many of the little crabs that made up much of our diet. There were no sea bird nests either, and I found nothing with which to supplement our supplies. I trekked back to the others, telling myself we had enough food with us, anyway. But Hennie's gloominess about the oracle had wormed into my brain, and I felt disheartened at not finding anything.

The others had built a fire while I was gone. It was a beacon, signalling that someone was here on the beach. Anyone tracking us would find us easily with the flames and the smoke to guide them. I wanted to smother it, but the breeze was brisk tonight and the one blanket apiece we had brought wouldn't be enough to keep us warm, even with the fire.

The night was long and cold, and my mood hadn't improved by dawn. I kept my mouth shut as we broke our fast and prepared to leave. If I said anything, it would likely be to snap at Seti, so it was better if I didn't speak.

We spent a second night on the beach, much to Seti's dismay, and it was the middle of the third day before we reached the place where the shore curved like a snake. A rock marked the middle curve, just as the woman who gave me directions had said. We set off inland from there. Half a league, she had said, to the fig tree cleaved in two by lightning.

"How much further?" Seti called from somewhere behind me.

I ignored her, too intent on searching for the fig tree.

"Tey, how far?" she called again.

We had gone more than half a league; I was sure of it. Had we missed it? Had we veered off in the wrong direction when we left the shore? I stopped and tried to figure out where we went wrong.

"Wait here," I said as the others caught up.

Seti flung herself to the ground with an exaggerated sigh.

I walked in a large loop around the place where they waited.

"Half a league," I muttered. "Aten damn it, I am sure that is half a league."

I found the fig tree eventually. The directions hadn't been very accurate. It was to the north-west, rather than the west, and more like two-thirds of a league. But there was a large fig tree, which was indeed split in two, and not very far away was the opening to a cave. I hurried back to the others.

It took twice as long to get back to the oracle's cave, and Seti asked at least a dozen times if we were almost there. I ignored her every time. Hennie tried to reassure Seti, but gave up when not even a minute passed before the girl asked yet again how much further we had to walk. At last, we stood in front of the cave.

"What do we do now?" Hennie whispered.

I shrugged. "The woman who gave me directions didn't say, only that the oracle chooses who she speaks with."

"Maybe we should sit out here and wait. If the oracle is genuine, she probably already knows we are here. If she wants to speak with us, she will come out."

I didn't like the idea of waiting without even knowing whether the oracle knew we were here, but I sat down. My legs were rather tired, anyway. I was so busy every day with searching for food or other things we needed to survive that it had been a long time since I trained properly. I was no longer as fit as I once was. I would resume my training as soon as we got home. I couldn't afford to risk being out of condition when our pursuers next caught up to us.

The scent of fire caught my attention and I spotted a trail of smoke rising into the sky. Presumably it came from within the cave, although I couldn't see the place it escaped from. It was dusk before the oracle came to the entrance. I had been about to suggest to Hennie that perhaps we should call out to her when she appeared.

I had expected a crone, but she was little more than a girl. Older than Nef, but several years younger than me. Thirteen perhaps, fourteen maybe. Old enough to marry. Surely too young to spend her life alone in a cave. She stood there for a full minute, silently observing us.

"Well, come in," she said at last. "Unless you intend to sit out here all night."

TWENTY-EIGHT

TEY

The oracle looked right at me as she spoke and I thought she intended for only me to enter. But Hennie and the girls rose, and the oracle didn't object when they followed me inside. She led us along a narrow, twisting tunnel, which opened into a large cave. I envied her entranceway, for the tunnel would mean no unwelcome breezes ever found their way inside.

Past the entrance, her cave didn't look all that much different from ours. Lamps gave plenty of light to see by and the smoke from a fire in a central hearth rose right up and out through a crevice in the roof. A bed mat and a pile of neatly folded blankets marked her sleeping area. A row of baskets against the wall held her supplies. Two buckets of water. Rugs to shield her from the coldness of the rocky floor. Even a few cushions. I found myself surprised at the homely touches. Whatever I had expected an oracle's home to look like, it wasn't this.

The oracle gestured to a rug beside the hearth.

"Sit," she said.

We sat in a row. The heat from the fire warmed my skin and I only now realised how chilled I felt. Seti was blessedly quiet, and I prayed she wouldn't complain in front of the oracle. The oracle knelt on a cushion in front of us. She raised her hands to cover her eyes and I glimpsed markings around her wrist. Snakes, maybe. At length, she uncovered her eyes and looked at me.

"You seek wisdom," she said.

That was hardly a message from the gods. Anyone who came to an oracle sought wisdom.

"You search," she said. "You run. You avoid the thing you most want because you do not even know you want it."

"I don't know what that means," I said.

"Listen to your heart," she said. "It will tell you."

She looked then at Hennie, but she only studied the woman and said nothing before turning her gaze on first Nef, then Seti. She examined each, but offered nothing further. Was that it? Was this the wisdom we had travelled so far for? Either she was finished or she waited for payment before she offered anything more. I retrieved a gem from my pouch. It was a pretty sapphire which sparkled in the firelight. The oracle looked at it, but made no move to take it.

"We came by this honestly." Perhaps she didn't take it because she thought we had stolen it. "It belonged to the girls' mother. It is part of their inheritance."

"Is that what the wisdom you seek is worth to you?" The oracle's voice was carefully neutral, and I got no sense of whether she approved or disapproved of my offering.

"Is there something else you would like?" I asked.

She looked deep into my eyes, but said nothing. Then she studied each of the others again. At last, she turned back to me.

"You will stay with me," she said. "Your family will leave and you will stay for a period of half a year. After that, I will give you the wisdom you came for and then you may return to your family."

I stuttered as I tried to find a response.

"I— But— We cannot be separated. We must stay together for the safety of the girls."

She shrugged and turned her gaze to the fire.

"That is my offer," she said. "Accept it or no."

"But how do we know you have the information we seek? You might not tell us anything useful."

"You doubt the wisdom of the gods?" She glanced at me, but if I had angered her, she hid it well.

"I doubt the ability of a mortal to perceive the wisdom of the gods," I said.

She turned back to the fire.

"As well you might," she said. "It is your choice, though. You may stay or go. Make your decision."

"Perhaps we should discuss this outside," Hennie said.

"No," the oracle said. "It is she who will stay and she who must decide."

"Tey, if she has information for us, we should take it," Hennie whispered.

The oracle could surely hear, but she kept her gaze on the fire and pretended she didn't.

"Three days ago you thought we shouldn't come and now you want me to stay here alone for six months?" I whispered back.

"She knows something. I feared we might come all this way and learn nothing, but she has information for us. Whatever it is, we need it."

"It is out of the question," I whispered back. "You know that."

"I don't think she would part us if she knew it would endanger the girls."

I shook my head, unwilling to say anything else in front of a stranger. Nef's eyes glistened as if she was about to cry. Seti looked from me to the oracle, her face calm enough that I suspected she didn't understand what we were talking about. I was wrong.

"I will stay," she said.

"Seti, no," Hennie said quickly.

"She is not staying," I said.

The oracle looked at Seti, a longer, harder look than before.

"You hunger," she said. "Guilt burns inside you. You offer to stay because you think I can appease those feelings."

"Can you?" Seti asked.

The oracle tipped her head to the side and studied her again.

"Perhaps I can, perhaps not. Regardless, it is not you the wisdom is intended for. There is someone who can help you better than I can."

"Who?" Seti asked. "Where?"

"A long way from here. You will find her when you least expect to."

"What does that mean?" Irritation crept into Seti's voice. "Just tell me who it is."

The oracle looked back at me. She had nothing further for Seti, it seemed.

"Well," she said. "Have you decided?"

"What if we gave you more than one gem?" I asked. "Would that be sufficient payment?"

I fished in my pouch and pulled out another. A scarlet ruby. I offered both gems on the palm of my hand. The oracle barely glanced at them before she shook her head.

"I have made my offer," she said.

"You do not understand what you ask of me," I said. "My duty is to keep them safe. There are people, perhaps many people, who would kill these girls as soon as they find them. There are others who want to use them. I cannot be separated from them. I am the only thing keeping them safe."

"Not the only thing, perhaps," the oracle said.

Her gaze strayed from me back to Seti.

"Can you at least give me some clue as to what information you have for us?" I asked. "Something to help me decide."

She tipped her head to the side, studying me. I was sure she would refuse.

"Danger comes for you," she said. "But you already know that."

"And you can tell us who is coming? Or when? I need something more specific."

She only looked at me and said nothing further.

"Please," I said. "Ask anything else of me. Give me another way to pay you and I will do it gladly, but I cannot risk being parted from the girls."

She looked at me for a long moment, then she raised her hands to cover her eyes again.

"Wait," I said.

Something inside me knew that once she repeated the action she had done at the start, our time with her would be over. I had only moments left in which to convince her.

"Please, I am their protector. I am the closest thing they have to a mother. I must be with them."

She didn't reply, only raised her hands again.

"I will do it," I said, before her hands reached her face.

She lowered her hands.

"But let me take them home first," I said. "It is a long way for them to travel alone and they might get lost. I will take them home and then come straight back to you. I will return in no more than five days."

"How do I know you will honour your promise?" the oracle asked.

"Are you not an oracle? Surely you can tell. Besides, if you will not give us your wisdom until I have spent six months with you, I have no other choice."

She studied me a while longer, then her gaze drifted down to my left hand.

"The ring," she said. "You may take them home, but you will leave your ring as surety. You may have it back when you return."

I ran my fingers over the ring.

"This was my mother's," I said. "It is the only thing I have of her and it is very precious to me."

The oracle only looked at me. I sighed and slipped the ring off my finger. It was the first time I had taken it off since my father gave it to me. I clutched it for a moment, then touched it to my lips before I offered it to her.

She slipped it into a pouch at her waist.

"It is late," she said, getting to her feet. "You may stay the night and leave at first light. I will expect you to return within five days." She gestured towards the buckets. "There is water if you wish to wash. Use the bucket on the left. The one on the right is for drinking. One of you can help me prepare food."

She began rummaging through her baskets of supplies.

I didn't notice Hennie come to stand beside me until she touched my hand.

"It will be worth it, Tey. We need to know what she knows."

"We should leave," I said. "Right now. We could walk away and not come back."

"And then we would not learn the wisdom she has for us and you would lose your mother's ring. We will stay the night as she has kindly offered and tomorrow you will take us home. Then you will return as you promised."

"But what about you and the girls? Who will protect you while I am here? Who will go to the village when you need supplies and do all the other the things I do? I cannot stay. It is ludicrous."

"We will manage because we must," Hennie said. "You agreed and you must keep your word."

"But what if her information isn't what she made it sound like? What if it is worthless to us?"

"I doubt that will be the case. You may not understand it when she first tells it to you, but that is the nature of an oracle's wisdom. They are always obscure, couched in riddles and mysteries. She may not even know what it means herself, but we will figure it out. If nothing else, now we know that those who pursue us will find us again. So we can prepare for that."

"And what if it happens while I am stuck here? I cannot leave you all for that long."

"You must, Tey."

TWENTY-NINE

SETI

I didn't quite understand what an oracle was. Nef thought it was someone who knew things. Special things nobody else knew. The whole time we were walking to find the oracle, I was praying to Aten the oracle would teach me how to make the bad thing listen to me.

I should stop calling it the bad thing, but I didn't know what else to call it. I had always called it that, right from when I first realised I was different to my sisters because I had something inside me that they didn't.

Tey was wrong when she said a god had put the bad thing inside me. If it was true, why would a god choose me? There was nothing special about me, not even that I was a princess. Maybe if I was the only princess in the world, but I had five sisters once and they were all princesses too. I wasn't even the oldest. I was nobody important.

THIRTY
TEY

The oracle was a gracious enough host, although it must have been startling for someone who lived alone to suddenly have four companions. I suggested I should sit up to keep watch, but the oracle said it wasn't necessary as she would know if anyone came near her cave.

I lay awake most of the night, wondering whether I had made the right decision. I dreaded leaving Hennie and the girls unprotected for so long, but if the oracle said she had wisdom for us but wouldn't give it until I had paid with my time, what other choice was there?

As we left her cave the next morning, my mood was dark. Hennie seemed preoccupied and even the girls said little. It was not until we reached the shoreline and turned back towards the village that Hennie spoke.

"Well, Tey," she said. "I am sure this does not sit easy with you, but I cannot see any other option. What are your thoughts now you have had the night to think about it?"

"Six months, Hennie. I cannot leave the three of you unprotected for so long. It makes me sick in the stomach to even consider it."

"Are we to travel all the way here only to learn that even though she has wisdom for us, you are not willing to pay the price? You thought this would be valuable, and it seems she does indeed have information about our pursuers. That is what you wanted. You must see us back to the cave and then return to her."

"How can I protect you if I am so far away?"

"Maybe we can move closer to you. A house in the village. We would be only a day's walk away."

"It is still too far," I said. "We should have asked if we could all stay. Perhaps we could have negotiated with her."

"She wants you, Tey. There must be a purpose to her request. It is not merely payment for services to be rendered. There is something else she wants from you."

"What?"

Hennie shrugged. "She will tell you in time. For now, I think you can only do as you have said you will."

Two days later, we passed the village without stopping, much to the girls' dismay. They wanted to see the market, but I didn't have time to spare if I was to return to the oracle within five days. I didn't want them seen in the village, anyway.

As we passed the last of the houses, I spotted a familiar figure turn to study us.

"Aten, no," I whispered.

"Tey?" Hennie asked.

He started towards us.

"Walk faster," I said.

She looked at the man headed for us.

"He does not look very threatening," she said. "And your blush tells me that is not what this is about."

"Just walk," I hissed and turned back to the girls who were dawdling some distance behind us as usual. "Neb, Sensen, hurry up. We have a long way to go yet today."

"Hello there," the man called as he approached. "I thought I recognised you."

I pretended I hadn't heard him.

"Hello," Nef called back.

"Neb," I hissed. "We do not know him."

Of course he heard me.

"My apologies," he said. "I never introduced myself the last time we met. My name is Tuthmose, and yes, before you ask, I am indeed named after Tuthmose the Third, may he live for millions of years. My father greatly admired him, although Pharaoh went to the West long before Papa was born."

"I am afraid we have no time to talk." I grabbed Hennie's arm and tried to push her along without looking like I dragged her. All three of them had stopped and were gawking at Tuthmose. "We really are in a hurry."

"Is your husband not with you?" Tuthmose asked. "Let me escort you back to him."

I couldn't decide whether to stick with our usual story about my husband being dead or to say I had none. Tuthmose seemed friendly, but he still might have been sent to search for us. Since the previous attempts to capture us hadn't succeeded, perhaps they were trying a new tactic.

"It is none of your business," I said finally, still unable to decide and realising I had to make some kind of reply. I tugged Hennie's arm. "Come on, we need to go."

"You are heading south?" Tuthmose asked. "I just came from that direction. You should know you won't be alone if you go that way. I mention it only because you seem like a woman who prefers to be alone."

I sighed and ignored his subtle dig at my rudeness. I couldn't *not* ask after that.

"Who will we encounter?" I asked.

"Soldiers," he said. "A whole squad of them."

"What are they doing?" My voice was sharper now and I hoped he didn't notice my alarm.

"Working their way along the coastline, it seems," Tuthmose

said. "I didn't speak to them. They were clearly on a mission and I prefer to stay out of the way of men like that."

"Let's go," I said to Hennie and the girls. "Now."

Before we could move, the squad came into sight. Tuthmose was right. They were indeed soldiers, well trained and alert. They walked in the manner of men accustomed to covering leagues in a day.

"What do we do?" Hennie whispered to me.

Tuthmose glanced at her, and I knew he had heard.

"We keep walking," I said. "Keep your heads down and let me do the talking."

I expected Tuthmose to sidle away, but he walked with us. I said nothing, too busy trying to think of how I might convince the squad we weren't who they searched for.

"Hello there," Tuthmose called as we came within speaking distance of the men. He had inserted himself between me and Hennie. "Fine day today, is it not?"

Considering he had wanted to avoid them, he was being awfully friendly. Suspicion flared within me. Did he deliberately lead us right to them?

The men stopped in front of us and I felt their hard stares as they looked us up and down, paying particular attention to Nef and Seti.

"My name is Tuthmose," he said. "This is my wife and my mother." He gestured to me, then Hennie. "My daughters." A nod towards the girls. "Just passing through, are you?"

"We are looking for two girls," one of the men said. "They were kidnapped and the family has hired us to retrieve them."

"I wish you much luck," Tuthmose said. "It would devastate me should something happen to one of our girls. We lost two others, you see. One didn't breathe after she was born and the other lived only a few months. So it has been precious for my wife and I to see these two girls of ours grow up."

He wrapped his arm around my shoulders and pulled me in against him.

"Hasn't it, love?" he asked me.

"Yes, of course." I lowered my gaze and tried to look like a good and docile wife who was not at all confused about what her "husband" was saying. "Very precious."

"Who are you?" Hennie screeched suddenly. "What are you doing here?"

"Mother, all is well." Tuthmose released me and took Hennie's arm. "They are just out for a nice walk on the beach."

"Who are you?" she screeched again. She flapped her arms up and down as if she thought they were wings and she was trying to take flight.

"She gets confused sometimes," Tuthmose said, turning back to the squad. He tapped the side of his head. "She does not react well to strangers. We try to avoid encountering anyone she doesn't know. It will take me hours to settle her again."

"Who are you?" Hennie cried even louder.

Tuthmose put his arms around her and seemed to try to calm her.

Since the soldiers were all watching Hennie and Tuthmose's performance, I went to the girls. With my back to the men, I put my arms around them and pretended I was trying to prevent them from seeing what was happening. Shielded from the men's view, I slipped a dagger from the sheath on my wrist.

"Nef, take this," I whispered as Hennie cried out again. "Don't look now, but there is a row of bushes to your right. If I tell you to run, go as fast as you can and get behind them. Stay there until I come to get you."

The girls' faces were white and I prayed they wouldn't ask questions the men might hear, but they only nodded.

"We need to be off," Tuthmose said to the men. "Enjoy your walk. Come now, Mother. Let's get you home."

He turned Hennie around and started back towards the village. I grabbed Nef and Seti's hands and hurried after him, keeping my gaze averted as I expected most women likely would after encountering a squad of soldiers. Hennie continued to cry out and only stopped when we reached the houses. Tuthmose glanced behind us.

"They are out of sight," he murmured. "I will take you to my home and you can rest there for a while."

He hurried us to a small cottage on the edge of the village. It was only once we were inside with the door locked that I felt like I could breathe again. Hennie sank onto a cushion, exhausted after her performance. The girls were pale and Nef's hand trembled as she passed me the dagger. I slipped over to the window and peered out. There was no sign of the men.

"Why did you do that?" I asked Tuthmose.

He frowned at me.

"Do what?"

"Pretend we were your family. Go along with it when Hennie pretended to lose her mind."

"You were in trouble and I was trying to help. From the way you reacted, I gathered you thought those soldiers were looking for you. Or if not you, perhaps someone with you."

He shot a meaningful look towards Nef and Seti.

"You don't know what you are talking about," I said.

"No, I don't. I couldn't possibly since you have not even given me your name. But those men looked like trouble, and when trouble travels with an entire squad in search of a young woman and her daughters, it is never a good thing. I could see no pleasant outcome for any of you if they decided it was you they were looking for."

I took a deep breath and tried to push away my mistrust. He wouldn't have helped us get away if he was sent to find us.

"Thank you," I muttered. The words didn't come easily. "And Hennie, that was very well done. How did you ever think of such a thing?"

Hennie beamed.

"I didn't really think about it," she said. "I just opened my mouth and it came out. Once I said it the first time, they looked so startled that I kept going. Then when Tuthmose played along, it was all the better. Thank you, sir," she said to him. "The ruse would not have been so effective if you had not pretended I was your senile old mother."

Tuthmose laughed.

"It was a wonderful performance and I was most happy to take part," he said. "Did you see the looks on their faces? They didn't know what to make of you and they only wanted to be away from us."

"We should do introductions," Hennie said. "I am Hennie. This is my daughter-in-law, Tentamun, and my granddaughters, Neb and Sensen."

At least she had used our cover names. We hadn't had cause to use them since we left the Sand Dwellers.

Tuthmose nodded to each of us as Hennie named us.

"I am most pleased to meet you," he said. "You should stay here for a couple of hours. The soldiers might linger in the village for a while, asking questions or whatever. We can have refreshments in the meantime."

I waited by the window as he fetched some drinks.

"Tentamun, please," he said, handing me a mug. "Sit down and rest. They were out of sight when we came in, so they will not know where you are."

I took the mug from him with a nod of thanks.

"I will keep watch," I said. "It does not hurt to keep an eye on what is happening outside."

He shrugged and returned to the rug where Hennie and the girls sat. As he lowered himself to join them, his back was to me and I tried not to notice the muscles in his shoulders. I had almost forgotten how he caught me looking at his chest the last time we met. My cheeks heated at the memory and I turned back to the window.

"We are keeping you from your work," Hennie said to Tuthmose. "What do you do?"

"Sailor," he said.

Surprised, I cast a look over my shoulder. I had picked him for a farmer, but a sailor would also have sun-darkened skin and hard muscles. Realising where my gaze had gone, I turned back to the window, taking a long drink of my beer to cover my discomfort.

"I thought a sailor would live in a harbour town," Hennie said.

I silently cheered her, pleased she hadn't just believed him without question.

"There is a town less than a day's walk to the north," Tuthmose said. "It is bigger than I am used to, though. I was born here and my family has always lived here. This is home. I come back between jobs."

His tone was easy and if he minded Hennie's question, he gave no sign of it.

"But how will you get another job if you are here rather than there?" Hennie asked. "Surely you would need to be where the ships are to secure work."

"When I run out of barley, I go back and look for more work," he said. "I don't need much to live on and I like to have a few weeks on land when I can. I am leaving again within the next day or two."

"And what happens with your house when you are away?"

Hennie's voice was studiously casual, but I knew what she was thinking.

"No," I said.

I gave Hennie a stern look, trying to convey the need for her to not say anything else. Tuthmose looked from Hennie to me.

"No, what?" he asked. "But to answer your question, my neighbour watches the house when I am away. Waters my vegetable garden when he remembers."

"Think how much better it would be if you had somebody living here while you are gone," Hennie said. "Somebody who could water your vegetables every day."

Tuthmose shot a look in my direction, as if expecting me to disagree. I kept my mouth shut. After all, I would be gone for months. If Hennie felt she and the girls would be safer here in the village, perhaps I should consider it. A senile old woman and her granddaughters might not draw much attention, especially if they kept to themselves.

"Well, yes," Tuthmose said. "But it would need to be someone I could trust. I wouldn't want to have someone here who might refuse to leave when I came home."

"Oh," Nef said. It was the first time either of the girls had spoken in front of Tuthmose. "We could live here while Mama is gone."

"Gone?" Tuthmose twisted around to look at me. "Where are you going?"

"I have business to attend to. For six months."

Not that I had decided to return to the oracle, but this opportunity might be worth exploring. We didn't have to agree to anything.

"I will be gone for a while," Tuthmose said. "Maybe less than six months. Maybe longer." He considered Hennie and the girls. "How far from here do you live?"

"Less than a day's walk," I said before anyone could offer more precise information. I still wasn't sure we could trust him, but this might be my best chance to keep them all safe while I was gone. If I went.

"You must be very isolated," Tuthmose said. "The nearest village in the direction you were headed must be another full day's walk past your home."

"We like to be alone," I said.

"But sometimes one can be too alone," Hennie said. "I do not relish the idea of being so far out of the village while Tentamun is away. If one of the girls is injured or ill and we need a physician, I would have to leave them alone for far too long to seek help."

"There is no physician in the village," Tuthmose said. "There are several healers, though. I am sure there is someone who could help with whatever you need."

He studied each of us again and sighed, as if he was having trouble deciding. Perhaps he wondered what he had gotten himself into.

"Fine," he said at last. "You may use the house while I am gone."

"Can I talk to you outside, Hennie?" I asked. "Girls, stay in here."

Tuthmose busied himself collecting our mugs while Hennie and I slipped outside.

"It is a good plan," she said before I could speak. "We will be far safer here than by ourselves in the cave."

"I don't trust him."

I wasn't sure that was true, though. Tuthmose had helped us, and he hadn't asked for anything in exchange. And now he had offered Hennie and the girls the use of his home.

"It will be good for the girls to have a proper roof over their heads for a few months," Hennie said. "Maybe they can even meet some other children. Perhaps attend school."

"No, no other children and no school. If you stay here, you must keep to yourselves. The more people who see the girls, the more chance someone will think to mention them next time men come searching."

"They have already checked this village and are not likely to return. They will keep moving up the coast."

"We don't know that, Hennie. Someone has seen enough to lead them this far. They know we are here. They might go a little further, but they will turn back eventually."

"And when that happens, it will be better for us to be here than by ourselves in the cave."

"I don't know, Hennie. Something about this doesn't feel right."

"You are too used to mistrusting people. Tuthmose has done nothing but help us. They would have captured us back there if not for him."

"And your marvellous screeching," I said. "I still cannot believe you did that."

Hennie chuckled.

"I cannot quite believe it myself, but it was the first thing I thought of," she said. "Most folk are uncomfortable with an old woman who appears to be mad. I didn't think they would want to get too close if I seemed to have lost my mind."

"You have to do it again if you encounter them a second time. It would seem strange if you didn't."

"Tey, don't worry about us. Go and do what you must. The girls and I will manage without you. I am well used to taking care of myself, after all. I lived alone for years before you three arrived on my doorstep."

I didn't respond, too busy wrestling with myself about the decision I needed to make.

"I know you believe you are the only one who can keep the girls safe, but as you can see, I am not quite as helpless as you thought," she said. "We will manage, Tey."

"I don't want to leave you. I feel like the oracle tricked us."

"Trick or not, it was the agreement we made and you must hold to it. Your Papa wouldn't want to think he had raised a daughter who doesn't keep her word."

The thought of Papa made my heart heavy. Was he still alive? We had been gone for more than two years. I could only pray Aten would keep him safe when his time came to journey through the underworld.

When we went back inside, the girls were playing a game with some wooden blocks. Tuthmose crouched beside them, offering advice.

"I made them for my son," he said, gesturing towards the blocks.

"You have a son?" I cast my gaze around the cottage. It comprised only a single chamber and I saw no evidence of either wife or child.

"He did not survive his birthing," Tuthmose said. "He went to the West and my wife with him."

"Oh." I didn't quite know what to say. It must have been painful for him to pretend we were his family. "I am sorry."

He shrugged. "It was several years ago. I try not to think about them too much."

"You must miss them."

"I barely knew my wife. Our parents arranged it and we were married for less than a year. Not long enough for us to learn to love each other. I loved my son, though. I would have tried to be a good father."

"You still could," I said. "You could marry again."

"I don't lead the kind of life that makes having a wife easy. Not when I am gone for months at a time. I would like children to come home to, but I am not so sure I would want a wife with them. What about you?"

After his honesty, I felt I had to give him something in return, even if I couldn't tell him the truth.

"I never wanted children," I said. "But I have two. Their father went to the West a couple of years ago. It is just the four of us now."

"Hmm," he said, and I wondered what he had learned that I hadn't meant to tell him.

"You have been very kind to us." Maybe flattery would distract him from the problem of my dead husband. "I appreciate the opportunity for Hennie and the girls to stay here while I am away."

"Where did you say you were going?"

"I don't think I did."

We looked at each other.

"It is a secret, then." His tone was light. "Some covert mission you are departing on."

"Something like that."

"You don't have to tell me, but you can trust me, Tentamun. I know you don't think you can."

"I didn't say I didn't trust you."

"You don't have to. I see it every time you look at me. Hear it in your voice. Hennie trusts me, but you don't."

"I am not used to trusting anyone," I said.

"You have the girls to look after, and with soldiers searching for them."

I shot him a look.

"What makes you think it was us they were looking for?"

"Two missing girls, supposedly stolen. You full of mistrust and secrets. And Hennie, who from what I have seen, is an articulate and completely sane woman, pretending to have lost her mind. It does not take a clever man to put those pieces together."

"I wish I could tell you more." The words were awkward on my tongue, but I thought they were true. "But it is not safe for anyone to know too much about us."

He only nodded.

"Do you need to return to your home?" he asked. "I assume you must have things you need to fetch. Clothes for the children or whatever."

"Yes, I should go. I can be there and back in a day if I leave early enough. If I may, I will leave the others here. I can travel faster alone."

"Go. They will be safe here with me while you are gone."

THIRTY-TWO

TEY

I left an hour before dawn and made it to our cave well before the sun was at its peak. I used the walk to figure out what I needed to collect and tried not to worry someone had found the cave while we were gone. But everything looked exactly as we left it and it took little time to sort through our things. A change of clothes each, extra blankets, the rest of our supplies. There wasn't anything else we needed which Tuthmose wouldn't already have. I spotted Seti's little wooden men as I was leaving and grabbed those too. The only thing we had of value was the pouch of gems and I kept that with me at all times.

I spent the walk back to Tuthmose's house worrying about what might have happened while I was gone. My heart thudded as the village came into sight and I barely refrained from running the rest of the way. I did walk a little faster, though, despite how tired my legs were from such a long walk with a heavy load. The girls were in the garden as I approached, although they had their backs to me and didn't notice my arrival. I burst into the cottage, startling Hennie as she swept the floor.

"Why are they outside alone?" I demanded, dropping my packs in the corner. "You should be watching them."

"Tey." Hennie's tone was mild, but I felt the sting of criticism.

"They are fine. They know to come in if anyone is nearby and, besides, they are not so far away that I won't hear if anything happens."

"They didn't even hear me enter the yard. I could have snatched them and been gone before you realised. "

"They need to be children. Children need time to play and mess around in the garden."

"You should still watch them," I said. "They can play outside as long as you supervise them."

"Tey, let them be children for a while. They have endured more than most girls their age."

"You know it is not safe."

I left her there and went out to the garden. The girls were wandering around, tracing a pattern through the grass. A dance, perhaps.

"Tey!" Nef was the first to notice me. She waved, although she didn't leave off her dance.

Seti glanced at me, but said nothing, seemingly too focussed on her footsteps to bother greeting me. I sat on the step to watch them and felt Hennie come up behind me.

"I am sorry," I said. "None of this is sitting well with me."

"We will be fine while you are gone. I feel so much better now we have a door that locks and we are close to help. You do not have to worry so much."

"I hate the thought of leaving them for so long. Before we went to the oracle, you were adamant we needed to stay together."

"I know, but I believe we have no other choice. We need whatever she can tell you, and the girls and I will manage without you if we must."

If our pursuers found them while I was gone, there would be nothing she could do to protect them.

"Hennie, if they find you, let them take the girls," I said.

"What? How can you say such a thing? You know I would never let them go without a fight."

"They will kill you without a second thought, and then they would take the girls, anyway. If they come, you should hide away. Pay attention to what they look like and what direction they leave in, then come find me. If I have enough information to track them, I will still have a chance of retrieving the girls."

"Tey, I love them as if they were truly Menna's daughters. I would gladly die if it would save them."

"That is my point. It won't save them. So, please, do as I say. If they come, hide away and get me as much information as you can."

Hennie took a long time to answer, but at length, she gave a heavy sigh.

"I cannot promise it," she said. "The situation might be such that I have no time to hide, but if I can, I will. That is the best I can give you."

I could only pray it would be enough.

Tuthmose returned shortly afterwards. He said little about where he had been, only that he had business to attend to and planned to leave the following day. I, too, would leave tomorrow. I had barely enough time to get back to the oracle within the five days she had specified.

Our evening meal was sombre, despite Hennie's attempts at festivity. Tuthmose said little, and I wondered whether he regretted allowing his home to be used or if it was the presence of the girls that bothered him. Seti kept trying to draw him into conversation and although he answered her, he made no other effort to talk.

I caught Hennie alone before bed and pressed a couple of gems into her hand.

"Keep these on your body at all times," I said.

She raised her eyebrows as she examined the gems.

"I assume these are from the girls' mother?" she asked. "I cannot take these, Tey. You should keep them with you. We will have no need of such a thing."

"Keep them. I want to know you have something valuable to trade if you need it."

I expected to toss and turn all night, but I was weary after walking to the cave and back, and fell into a deep sleep. I woke just before dawn and lay listening to the sounds of the others sleeping around me. The girls lay between Hennie and me, and Tuthmose was on the other side of the chamber. Nef moaned and her head jerked from side to side — a nightmare, perhaps. Both girls had them now and then. It was hardly surprising after all they had experienced.

I gave up trying to sleep and went to sit in the garden where I settled myself with my back against a dom palm and watched the sky grow orange in the east. Tuthmose came out just as the sun peered over the horizon.

"I wondered where you were," he said. He leaned against the dom palm.

"I was awake and didn't want to disturb anyone," I said.

"I know leaving them weighs heavily on you. It is obvious someone is looking for your family. I am not asking you to tell me your secrets, only reminding you I could help if you would share your burden."

"You cannot help." My tone was curter than he deserved. "Nobody can. This burden is mine and mine alone."

"It would seem it is Hennie's also, is it not? She is your husband's mother, and those girls are her granddaughters."

So he suspected Hennie wasn't who we claimed she was. We should have come up with a cover name for her. At least he didn't know her full name.

"As you say, they are her granddaughters," I said. "I would not have involved her if it could have been avoided, and I won't involve anyone else."

"I feel like I am involved anyway, given they will be living in my house. I only wish I knew exactly what I am involved in."

I didn't respond. He could ask as many times as he wanted and I would still tell him nothing.

"Tentamun, I know you are leaving for six months and this is probably the last thing you want to hear, but I need to say this before you go."

My heart pounded and I didn't want to hear whatever it was.

"Don't," I said. "If it will make things more complicated, don't say it."

He crouched beside me and reached for my hand. I pulled it away and clutched my hands together in my lap.

"There is something between us," he said. "I have never felt like this with anyone else. I told you my father chose my wife and I never loved her. But I feel like you and I—"

I got to my feet.

"Stop it," I said. "There is nothing between us. I appreciate you giving Hennie and the girls the use of your home, but that doesn't mean there is anything between you and me. We can pay you, if that is what you want, but it will not be with my body."

He, too, rose to his feet. I avoided looking at him, but I couldn't miss the hurt in his voice.

"I wasn't suggesting any such thing," he said. "And I am sorry if that is what you thought. I will say nothing further of it, since it is clear you don't feel the same way."

He left me and walked off down the street. I let him go, even though something inside me said I should chase after him. I should grab his hand and make him stop and… That was where my thought ended. I didn't know what I wanted to do after that. I didn't know what I wanted from him.

THIRTY-THREE
TEY

Tuthmose didn't return before I left and nobody comment on his absence, although Hennie shot me more than one concerned look. Perhaps she had woken in time to overhear part of our conversation, or perhaps she merely sensed something had happened between us. Our farewells were brief, and soon I was on my way back to the oracle.

It was almost sunset when I reached the winding stretch of shoreline and found the rock marking where to turn inland. I considered spending the night on the beach and going to the oracle in the morning, but my feet just kept walking. There was little light left by the time I approached her cave and at first I didn't see her standing at the entrance.

"So," she said as I stopped in front of her. "You have returned."

"Did you think I wouldn't?"

She cocked her head to the side and studied me.

"Follow me," she said.

She led me along the winding tunnel and into the cave. A fire blazed in the central hearth, casting a cheery glow over its surroundings. A pot set to the side gave off a fishy aroma.

"I thought you would be hungry." The oracle gestured towards the pot. "You may help yourself."

"I don't even know your name," I said as I put down my packs. "If I am to live here with you, will you tell me what you are called?"

"Oracle will be sufficient. It is what everyone else calls me."

"But you must have a name. What did your mother call you?"

She didn't look at me.

"That name is long forgotten."

"It cannot be that long. You are younger than me."

She sat beside the hearth, her long legs folding gracefully beneath her.

"Tey, you are here to learn and to serve. I do not intend to tell you my life story."

"I never told you my name."

She looked at me, the arch of her eyebrows suggesting amusement.

"And yet I know it, anyway. In truth, I wasn't sure that was correct. I couldn't quite tell whether it was Tey or Ten."

"I go by both," I muttered.

A low stool near the hearth bore a bowl, a ladle, and my mother's ring. I slipped the ring back onto my finger. Had I not returned, losing that ring would have hurt more than I cared to admit. I served myself some soup from the pot. It was bland and would have benefitted from a handful of herbs, but I was hungry and it would nourish my body regardless of whether I found it tasty. Oracle seemed content to sit silently while I ate.

"So, are you going to tell me why I am here?" I asked as I set my bowl aside, my hunger sated.

"You are paying for my wisdom," she said. "You already know this."

"Does everyone who seeks wisdom come to live with you?"

"Of course not."

"Then why me?"

"Why you, Tey? Why you indeed."

I waited, but she said nothing further.

"What does that mean?" I asked. "I need to know what you want from me."

"Your time, Tey. You will pay for my wisdom with your time."

"But that is the thing I can least afford."

She didn't reply.

"How much do you know about me?" I asked.

"Little. What I see of you is confusing. It is as if you are two people at once. Or one who pretends to be someone else."

She knew more of the truth than I expected. I had thought that if she knew anything, it would only be the future, not me.

"What will I be doing here?" I asked.

"We will start tomorrow," she said. "I am going to sleep now."

She rose just as gracefully as she had sat down and retrieved her bed mat from where it waited, neatly rolled and leaning against the cave wall. She spread it beside the fire, pulled a blanket over herself, and closed her eyes. Not knowing what else to do, I followed her example.

I slept little that night. Oracle's cave felt different to our own, and I already worried about Hennie and the girls. Could we trust Tuthmose or was he only waiting for me to leave before he did something? What he might do, I couldn't have said. It was just a vague feeling of worry, and maybe it was nothing more than that I didn't like not having control over the situation. I tried to forget his words about there being something between us, but they refused to stay buried.

I wasn't sure what I had expected Oracle's life to be like, but it wasn't all that different to life in our own cave. She rose at dawn when sunlight filtered in through the crevice in the roof. She fetched water and scavenged what food she could from the surrounding area. She spoke little, preferring to gesture when she wanted something from me. I quickly learned to interpret her commands, and the silence suited me just fine.

I had been living in her cave for a week before she had any visitors.

"There is a woman coming to see me today," Oracle said as we broke our fast in front of the hearth. "You may stay and observe, but keep out of the way and do not speak."

"She comes to seek your wisdom?"

"Of course."

"How do you know she is coming today? Did she send a message?"

"I always know when someone seeks me."

"But how?"

She scraped the remains of last night's soup from her bowl and didn't look at me.

"You should not be so quick to dismiss what you do not understand, Tey."

"I wasn't dismissing it. I was asking how you knew."

She didn't answer, only rose to rinse her bowl in the bucket of washing water.

"If you go now, you will have time to fetch water before she arrives," she said. "She will be here within the hour."

The creek lay some distance behind the cave and as I returned, I saw a woman wandering rather aimlessly. She waved and hurried towards me. If this was the one Oracle expected, she had gone right past the cave. Had Oracle sent me to find water knowing I would also find the woman? Was this her way of showing me she knew more than she said?

"Are you the oracle?" the woman called as she approached.

Surely I looked nothing like one would expect of an oracle.

"I can take you to her," I said.

She chattered nervously as we walked.

"Thank you for taking me. I think I got a little lost. The instructions seemed rather vague, and I really wasn't sure I could find the cave. Do you live with the oracle? I thought she lived alone. I have never heard mention of someone living with her."

I tuned her out and concentrated on not spilling the water.

Oracle was waiting at the cave entrance when we arrived. I hung back as she greeted the woman, uncertain whether I should go in. Oracle gave me a small nod and I assumed that meant to follow them. I set the buckets down as soon as I reached the cave, rather than taking them over to their usual spot, fearing I would spill the water and interrupt. Not knowing what else to do with myself, I sat beside the buckets.

Oracle gestured for the woman to sit on the rug by the hearth, then knelt on her cushion in front of it. She held out her hand and the woman passed her the bag she carried. Her payment, I guessed. Oracle set the bag aside without looking inside it. She raised her hands to cover her eyes, just as she had when we sat there. But before she could speak, the woman began to talk.

Her sister was with child, it seemed, and she believed neither her sister nor the child were well. She wanted to know what would happen to her sister, and to her sister's other children if the woman went to the West. It seemed the sister's husband had run off and as they had no other family, she feared being stuck raising their children herself. The woman spoke for some time before she fell silent. I wondered that she seemed to think Oracle needed to be told all that. It was only once she stopped that Oracle spoke.

"The ocean's tide is strong," she said. "Let only the strongest swimmer venture far from shore. The others should wait. Their purpose lies elsewhere."

Hennie had said her wisdom would be obscure, and I could make no sense of it. Oracle raised her hands to cover her eyes again, signalling the end of the wisdom. Then she nodded at the woman and gestured for her to leave. As the woman passed me, I glimpsed her face. She seemed calmer now, satisfied with the wisdom she had received. I wondered whether she made any more sense of it than I could.

Once she had gone, I moved the buckets to where they usually stood.

"What will happen to her sister?" I asked. "I didn't under-stand what you told her."

Oracle shrugged. "The wisdom is for her, not me."

"You mean you don't understand it yourself? Then why do

you say such things? Why don't you tell them something that makes sense?"

"Because then it would not be the wisdom," she said. "I pass the wisdom on exactly as I receive it. It matters not whether I understand it. She will make sense of it in time."

"But where does it come from?"

"From the goddess, of course." She gave me a puzzled look. "Where did you think it came from?"

I shrugged and busied myself with sweeping the cave floor, which had become one of my daily chores. Oracle wanted it swept every day, although it hardly seemed to need it. Still, she had said I was here to serve and learn, so serve I did. It wasn't until the following day that it occurred to me to ask which goddess she meant.

"Ma'at," Oracle said. She gave me a look that suggested she didn't understand why I needed to ask.

"I don't know much about her."

"The old gods are not as forgotten as some might think," Oracle said. "Especially not for those of us who receive their wisdom."

I had heard of Ma'at, but I knew little other than that her Feather of Truth would provide the balance to the scales on which my heart would be weighed when I went to Osiris's Hall. Papa said Egypt used to worship many gods and goddesses — hundreds at least, perhaps even thousands — before Pharaoh Akhenaten decreed we could worship only Aten.

Aten was who I had grown up with and he was all I knew. What would it be like to have lived in an earlier time when people worshipped whichever god they chose? Did children learn of different gods at school? Was a child expected to worship the same god as their father in the way sons expected to follow their father's trade?

I prayed to Aten that Oracle's wisdom would be worth the six months she demanded from me and that we would be safer after this. That we would know exactly who pursued us and when they would come. That we could find a place to settle down where the girls could have a normal life again. Maybe they would even have the chance to choose a god for themselves. I felt disloyal at suggesting such a thing to Aten, and pushed the thought out of my mind.

THIRTY-FOUR

SETI

Tey would be gone for a really long time. It would be just Nef and Grandmother and me and the bad thing, and we would all live in Tuthmose's house. Tey wasn't happy about it. She wanted us to go back to the cave where it was cold and we weren't anywhere near a market to get food. I liked it here at Tuthmose's. We had a proper house, even though it was really little and nothing like the palace. It had only one chamber, but it was bigger than the tent we lived in with the tribe.

I hardly remembered the palace anymore. It was big, I knew that. Nef and I shared a bedchamber, but I didn't really remember what it looked like. I couldn't remember our sister's face, Ankhesenpaaten, who Tey said was now called Ankhesenamun. I could see my father's face in my mind, but not my mother's. It made me sad I was forgetting them. It probably meant I was a bad daughter and a bad sister. A good daughter would remember what her mother looked like, even years after she had gone to the West.

When I was much littler, Tey told me we would have a house again one day, although it wouldn't be as big as a palace, and she and Nef and I would have to share a bedchamber. I couldn't remember whether she said where Grandmother would sleep, but maybe that was before we found her. I supposed it didn't really matter whether it was Tey or Grandmother who shared the bedchamber with Nef and me. There were still three of us, like Tey said.

She also said we would have bed mats and baths and hot dinners. We had those things when we lived in the cave. Well, not proper baths. Nef and I bathed in the stream, but sometimes Tey brought a bucket of water for Grandmother to heat in her pot on the fire. Grandmother liked to have a warm bath, even if it wasn't a proper bath you could sit in. She just got a cloth and wiped herself all over with warm water, but she seemed happy enough with that.

So we finally had a house again and everything would be better now. Or that was what I thought until Tuthmose came home and said we had to leave.

THIRTY-FIVE

TEY

The days and weeks passed, each much the same as the one before. Folk came seeking Oracle's wisdom every week or two, and it seemed this was where most of her supplies came from. They brought loaves of bread or baskets of vegetables from their garden. Lengths of linen or a woven blanket. Oracle accepted each offering graciously, no matter how small. One woman brought only a single onion.

"Surely that is not enough," I said after she left. "The man who came last week brought you a blanket. Why would you accept one onion in payment?"

"That was as much as she could afford," Oracle said. "That makes her onion just as valuable as the blanket. Each person brings what they can afford. That is all I ask."

"Then why did you ask for six months from me? You knew I couldn't afford that. We had other ways we could have paid you."

"Ahh, but as it turns out, you can afford six months, can you not? You would not be here otherwise. And your time is far more valuable to you than anything else you might have offered. To you, it is as valuable as the onion was to its giver."

I tried not to worry about Hennie and the girls, and instead to keep my mind focussed on the tasks Oracle gave me. But much of what she asked of me was mindless and repetitive, leaving my thoughts with too much time to wander. She wanted the leaf of a particular shrub — many, many leaves — and I spent days searching the surrounding landscape to find enough of them.

Another time, she wanted the threads of a blanket separated so she could use the wool for some other purpose. I painstakingly pulled the blanket apart, although it seemed a shame to ruin such a fine item. It bore an intricate design of a circle with a straight line coming off it and a smaller circle in its centre. I couldn't figure out what it was supposed to represent and Oracle only shrugged when I asked if she knew.

I stripped the leaves and carefully sliced every last thorn off a long, tangled length of vine she intended to use as rope. The thorns pricked me so many times the vine was streaked with my blood long before I finished.

The tasks Oracle gave me were so strange that I suspected they must hold more meaning than I comprehended. Perhaps they were somehow part of the wisdom I was paying for. So I tried to keep my mind on my tasks and to pay careful attention to them. If these tasks contained the wisdom I had come in search of, I didn't intend to squander it.

"Tell me," I said one evening after we had eaten our meal. We sat together on the rug in front of the fire. Oracle and I had formed a relationship of sorts, although each of us continued to hold tight to our own secrets. "How did you come to be here, living in a cave by yourself?"

She was silent for a long while and I thought this would be one of those questions she never answered. I had given up waiting and was absorbed in my thoughts before she replied.

"As a child, I was different." Oracle spoke haltingly, as if unused to explaining this to anyone. "I always knew I was different, although if you had asked me how, I couldn't have told you. But as I grew older, I came to realise the goddess spoke to me. That she gave me wisdom which she intended for me to share."

"Ma'at," I said.

"Yes, Ma'at. At first I tried to offer the wisdom to those I believed she intended it for, but folk would get angry with me. They would yell at me or slam the door in my face. One woman became so overwrought that she screamed at me until I left. Another time, a man grabbed my arm so hard, the bone snapped."

She raised her hand to touch her right wrist. I had noticed she didn't make full use of that arm and had assumed she simply favoured the other. But a broken bone that was never properly set would cause ongoing pain.

"So you decided to live alone in a cave?" I asked. "Wouldn't it have been easier to stop sharing your wisdom if folk didn't want it?"

She shot me a sideways glance before returning her gaze to the fire.

"Sometimes we must follow the path intended for us, regardless of whether it is what we would have chosen for ourselves or not. I would have thought you, Tey, of all people would understand this."

"What makes you think I follow a path that is not of my choice?"

The edges of her mouth turned up slightly.

"Always so defensive," she said. "You keep much to yourself. I think you and I are not so different."

I stopped myself before I argued with her. Oracle thought she and I were alike. Hennie thought Seti and I were alike. Why couldn't I just be me without people thinking I was like someone else?

"Why a cave, though?" I asked.

"At first, I just wanted to get away from the people gossiping about me. Folk fear what they do not understand and some of the rumours they spread were vicious. I came to live here, thinking to keep myself apart from everyone else. But one day, a young couple came to see me. The woman wanted to know if I had any wisdom for her. So I told her what Ma'at told me and they left.

Some time after that, someone else came. And ever since, folk come to me when they want to hear the wisdom. Those that don't, stay away. It suits all of us."

"Do you ever get lonely, being here by yourself?" I asked.

"Sometimes," she admitted, much to my surprise.

I hadn't expected she would answer, or if she did that it wouldn't be the truth. But then I had never known her to say anything other than the truth.

"I would have liked to have married," she continued. "Children, a house of my own. A family. I wanted to, oh, I don't know. You will think it stupid."

"I won't."

"I wanted to bake bread and mend my husband's clothes. I wanted to soothe my children when they were sick and laugh at their antics when they played."

Somehow, I didn't think I needed to tell her I wanted none of that. I suspected she already knew.

"Why can you not still have that?" I asked. "You are young enough to bear children yet."

"Because that is not my path. The goddess has chosen me to share her wisdom and in order for me to comprehend it, I need silence and contemplation. It is not a life that allows for a family."

"Me being here must be a problem for you, then."

It had never occurred to me that maybe she wanted me here as little as I did. Yet it was her decision that this was the only payment I could give her. Fears about Hennie and the girls slid into my brain and I resolutely pushed them away. I could do nothing for them here and I would only drive myself mad if I let myself worry about them.

"Somewhat," Oracle said. "But you needed to do this. It is the only way you would understand the wisdom."

"What do you mean?"

But she turned back to the fire and didn't speak again.

THIRTY-SIX

TEY

I kept careful track of the days, scraping a charcoal mark on a piece of bark each evening before I went to sleep. Five full months had passed — more than a season — and I was no closer to understanding what Oracle wanted of me than when I arrived. Serve and learn, she had said. I had certainly served, but if she had intended me to learn something specific, it seemed I had failed.

"I have only one month left," I said to her that evening.

We sat in our usual places on either side of the hearth while we ate. The husband and wife who came today brought two perch and Oracle had made a soup with them. I would have preferred to roast them over coals, but Oracle ate almost everything as a soup. She had a bad tooth, which made chewing too painful. Between that and her arm, which had been broken and not set properly, she must pass every day in agony.

"I know," she said.

"Is there something I should learn in the time I have left?"

She spooned more soup into her mouth before replying.

"You will."

"But what? What is it I am supposed to learn? I spend all day doing these tasks you set for me, but I am no closer to understanding why you wanted me here."

"Are you not?"

Her face was expressionless, and I couldn't tell what she was thinking. I was certain these seemingly mindless tasks she gave me must have some purpose, but whatever it was still eluded me.

"You have a month left," Oracle said. "There is time for you to learn if you have not done so yet. But I suspect you will find you have learnt more than you realise."

Oracle allowed me one hour to myself each day and I spent that time maintaining my fitness. I ran at least a league every day carrying a rock in each hand. I climbed trees to keep my arms strong and tracked hares through the undergrowth to sharpen my skills. By the time I returned to the cave, I would be sweaty and panting, but at least my mind was still. When I trained was the only time my mind calmed.

"One week," I said to Oracle the next time I raised the matter. "Ten days. That is all I have left."

"It is," she said.

"I still don't know what you wanted me to learn."

"You will see." She didn't sound at all concerned. "You worry too much."

On my last day with Oracle, I woke well before dawn, but I stayed on my bed mat, not wanting to disturb her. The fire had died down overnight and only a few coals remained, casting little light on the cave. Oracle shifted beneath her blanket and I realised she was already awake.

"Well, Tey." Oracle sat up and studied me as I folded my blanket and rolled my bed mat. "You have served your six months."

And yet I still have no idea what you wanted from me, I wanted to say, but I held my tongue. I would be back with Hennie and the girls by nightfall. I busied myself with shoving my blanket into a pack and didn't answer. We ate the rest of last night's soup. I was longing for something that wasn't soup. Maybe Hennie would have fresh bread ready when I returned. She and the girls would be keeping as careful note of the days as I did. They would know to expect me today. When I was ready to leave, Oracle followed me along the winding tunnel to the cave entrance. We stepped outside and I turned to face her.

"Will you give me your wisdom now?" I asked.

She raised her hands to cover her eyes and my heart pounded. I was afraid to hear what she had to say. There was a reason she wanted six months from me and I was about to learn it.

"Danger comes," Oracle said. "And it will be the catalyst who determines how events will proceed. If the catalyst does not wake in time, all four of you will die."

"Who is the catalyst?"

She lowered her hands from her eyes and looked at me steadily.

"You ask the wrong question."

"What question should I ask?"

She only continued to look at me.

"Has the catalyst woken yet?" I asked.

She raised her eyebrows, and I got the sense that this was the question she had waited for.

"Not yet," Oracle said. "And the time has come. The only question now is whether the catalyst will awake in time to save the lives of herself and those she loves."

I dropped my packs and ran.

My heart thudded as I pushed myself to go faster, faster. Why was Oracle's cave so far from Tuthmose's house? I couldn't afford to spend a whole day getting there. I ran until I couldn't run anymore, then I walked for a while, just long enough to catch my breath, before I ran again. Oracle's words repeated in my mind over and over. *Danger comes and it will be the catalyst who determines how events will proceed. The only question now is whether the catalyst will awake in time to save the lives of herself and those she loves.*

Rather than being obscure like Hennie had feared, the wisdom was clear enough. The catalyst was me. There was nobody else it could be. My time with Oracle must have served as an awakening of sorts. Our pursuers had found Hennie and the girls. It was only a matter of whether I could get there in time to save them.

By noon, I had reached the village.

As I approached Tuthmose's house, it was obvious something was wrong. The front door was open and it hung crookedly. Hennie's eyesight was poor, but even she would notice a broken door and arrange its repair, for the sake of the girls' safety, if nothing else.

I skirted the house, keeping out of sight of the doorway, and pressed myself against the back wall. There were no noises from inside and the shutters were closed, so I would know nothing until I went in.

I took a deep breath and prepared myself. They might still be there, perhaps guarded by soldiers. They might be gone. Or I might find their bodies.

With one last breath and a dagger in each hand, I burst through the door.

The house had been ransacked. Baskets upended, blankets torn, supplies strewn on the floor. No bodies, no blood. The place was such a mess that I couldn't tell whether there had been a struggle. Perhaps nobody was home when this happened. Perhaps they had already fled.

I pawed through the mess, trying to figure out whether anything was missing. It might indicate Hennie and the girls had gotten away before our pursuers arrived. I thought Hennie's spare clothes were gone, but they might be torn to pieces and scattered around the chamber. I found a sandal that might be Seti's, but perhaps she had gotten new shoes in the time I was away. She was still at an age where her feet were growing. A thick layer of sand covered everything, probably blown in through the open doorway. It had been weeks since anyone was last here. Months maybe.

I went to the next house and pounded on the door. I heard footsteps inside, but the door didn't open.

"Hello?" I called. "May I speak with you?"

The window shutters parted and a pair of dark eyes peered out at me.

"I have a question about the people who were living next door," I said.

The shutters closed and the door opened, just enough for me to see the woman inside. She clutched a babe to her breast.

"Do you know where they went?" I asked.

The woman's face was pale and her eyes regarded me fearfully.

"Nobody lives there anymore," she whispered. "Not even Tuthmose."

"There was an old woman and two girls staying there. Do you know what happened to them?"

"Soldiers came. From the noise, they must have broken everything in the house."

"Do you know if anyone was home at the time?"

"No screaming or shouting. But I don't know what happened. I locked the door and closed my shutters."

"When?"

She shrugged. "Maybe six months."

Six months. It had happened not long after I went to Oracle. Maybe even the same day. Had she known this would happen? Had she deliberately separated me from them? Did this have something to do with the awakening she thought I would experience?

There didn't seem to be anyone at home in the house on the other side of Tuthmose's. I returned and searched the house more thoroughly. Their bed mats were still there. I found enough pieces of blanket that none seemed to be missing. There were no shoes other than Seti's sandal and no sign of the gems I gave Hennie, but I had told her to keep them on her at all times. Beneath the remains of a broken chair, I found one of the little wooden men Seti took from Hennie's home. I had brought all three from the cave, but I couldn't find the others.

The only thing that made me think they might have fled —

maybe without time to take anything with them — was the absence of blood. The men pursuing us might take the girls back to Akhetaten, but they wouldn't bother to take Hennie as well. They would simply kill her and leave her here. So, with no bodies or blood, I had to assume she had managed to get away with the girls. The only question was, where did they go?

THIRTY-SEVEN

TEY

It was me who was the catalyst. Me who hadn't awoken in time to prevent whatever happened here. But how was I supposed to have known when Oracle wouldn't give me her wisdom until I had served the six months she required? Frustration and resentment warred within me and I tried to push the emotions away. They would only cloud my mind and would do nothing to help me find Hennie and the girls. Later, once I knew they were safe, would be time enough to wonder how I might have pieced together the clues from Oracle's tasks.

As the sun set, my stomach growled fiercely. I hadn't eaten since this morning. I found a couple of onions in the remains of Tuthmose's belongings. They were old, but would do me for tonight. I stood in the doorway as I ate, trying to figure out where Hennie might go if they had fled. We should have agreed on a destination before I left. Somewhere safe they could go if they needed to.

I tried to recall whether Hennie had ever mentioned a place that was special to her, or somewhere she would like to see. She had lived in Nubet all her life and had no reason to venture outside the town as far as I knew. The girls had never expressed interest in going anywhere other than back to Akhetaten. I could think of nowhere the three of them might flee to.

I was too worried to sleep and spent the night prowling the house. I pawed through the remnants of Tuthmose's things, and those of Hennie and the girls. Did Tuthmose even know his house had been ransacked? Surely if he had returned at any point since then, he wouldn't leave it like this.

I knew it was a bad idea for them to stay in the village. There were too many opportunities for people to see them. Too many chances that someone asking around about a pair of missing girls would stumble on a neighbour or someone who had seen them at the market. I should have insisted they stay in our cave. They would have been safer there.

Dawn arrived as I leaned against the wall beside the window. I had spent the night searching every cubit of the cottage and still hadn't found any blood. They had fled, I was sure of it. I just had to figure out where.

The broken window shutters wouldn't open, so I pulled them down and set them on the floor. As the early morning sunlight streamed in, I noticed something I hadn't seen before. The shutters had concealed a charcoal drawing on the windowsill. The images had been made in haste, the lines uneven.

A small circle inside a larger circle with a line leading off it. I had spent so long unpicking that Aten-damned blanket of Oracle's that I recognised the image immediately. It couldn't be a coincidence. Beside it was something that might have been a pair of legs, followed by four parallel lines. Papa had taught me to read a little, but I couldn't make any sense of this message.

Tuthmose had no papyrus in his home, but outside I found a broken mud brick. Using a piece of charcoal from the oven, I carefully copied the images onto the brick. Then I went back to see the woman next door.

"It is me again," I called through the door. "We spoke yesterday. You told me about the soldiers."

The door didn't open this time, although I could hear her

breathing just on the other side. The babe fussed and she whispered to it.

"Can you tell me where to find a scribe?" I asked. "Or a teacher."

Silence.

"Please," I said, more quietly. "They have taken my daughters. I need someone who can read."

The door opened just the tiniest bit and she peered out.

"If I tell you, promise you will not come back here again," she whispered. "I don't want them to think I am associated with you. I have to protect my own babe."

"Tell me and you will not see me again."

"Go to the west end of the marketplace. There is a street that leads away from it. The teacher lives in the third house. It has a blue door and is very fine."

The door closed.

I found the teacher's house, but only his wife and two young girls were at home. She frowned and seemed reluctant to tell me her husband was at work. Of course, he would be at school at this time of morning. She refused to tell me where the school was, saying I would get her husband in trouble if I pestered him there. So I went back to the marketplace and asked around until I found someone who told me where it was.

It was a mud brick building a little larger than a house, but comprising only one chamber. The boys sat in orderly rows, wooden writing tablets and charcoal set in front of them. A boy of about nine years old stood at the front of the class reciting something. The man beside him must be the teacher. He glanced up and noticed me standing in the doorway.

"If you wish to enrol a child, come back after lessons are finished for the day," he said sternly.

"I only have a question." I held the mud brick out to him. "Can you read this for me?"

He came to the door with a sigh and took the brick, although he only glanced at it before offering it back to me.

"It is impossible to tell without context," he said.

"Please, I need to know what it says."

"Where is the rest of the inscription? I cannot tell you what a couple of isolated symbols mean. I would need to see the entire passage."

"This is the whole message. Is there anything you can tell me?"

He frowned at the brick.

"I do not recognise the first symbol," he said. "The second is something to do with travel. *Come*, perhaps. The last might be the number of travellers. Without the rest of the inscription, I cannot interpret anything more."

I thanked him and left. Even though he couldn't translate it, he had given me enough to believe they fled the house with a plan of where they were going. The first image — the circles and the line from Oracle's blanket — must be their destination. The second meant *come to this place*. And the four lines told me four people had fled: Hennie, the girls, and someone else, probably Tuthmose. How had Oracle known the image of the circles and the line would be significant for me? And what was the purpose of all those hours I spent unpicking her blanket? What use was recognising the image if I didn't know what it meant?

I doubted Hennie could read any better than me, as only the girls of rich families endured any schooling. Nef and Seti would have had private tutors and could surely read and write at least a little. Perhaps one of them left the message. But what did the first picture mean?

I showed the brick to folk in the marketplace, hoping someone might interpret the two circles and the line. They all shook their heads or gave me blank looks. When I ran out of people to ask, I found a shady spot to sit and think about what to do next. I had only been there for a few minutes when an old man came to sit beside me.

"Mind if I share your shade?" he asked in a watery voice.

"Of course." I moved over to give him room.

"Too hot today for these old bones to be wandering around."

"Are you waiting for someone?" I asked.

He nodded towards a stall.

"My wife. She needs an escort when she comes to the market or she is likely to buy far too much and deplete my meagre savings."

"Do you know what this mark means?" I showed him the brick.

He took it from me and held it close to his face to examine it. He cleared his throat.

"Never seen it before."

We sat in silence after that.

"Been thinking," he said a few minutes later. "About places where folk might know about pictures like that."

"Yes?"

"A temple. Or an archive."

"Where would I find one of those?"

"Not here," he said. "A bigger village. You want to go to a city. Wherever Pharaoh lives these days, that is where you will find an archive."

THIRTY-EIGHT
TEY

Hope swirled within me as I made my way back to Tuthmose's house. I had proof they were alive, or at least they were at the time they fled. Whoever made that symbol thought I would understand it, or that I would figure it out.

I couldn't risk going to Akhetaten, but maybe I could try Thebes. Other pharaohs had lived there previously so there must be an archive somewhere in the city. But it would take weeks to get there and by then they might have moved on and their trail could be cold. There must be another way. The afternoon dragged as I paced the house. They thought I would understand their message. What was I missing?

It came to me late in the night. I didn't fall asleep until well after midnight, and I woke with a start, realising what I had missed. It might not have been Hennie or one of the girls who made those marks. It could have been Tuthmose. And Tuthmose was a sailor. If I wanted to learn what a sailor knew, I needed to find other sailors. I would go to the harbour town where the ships departed from. It was north of here, Tuthmose had said. About a day's walk.

I got up an hour before dawn. There was no point in waiting

longer. I wouldn't find Hennie and the girls by lying around. I copied the images from the windowsill onto a flat piece of bark which would be lighter to carry than the brick. Then I wrapped it in a piece of linen and hoped it would protect the images from getting smudged.

As I walked, my mind was free to torment me with thoughts of what might have happened. Hennie must have thought our pursuers were close and that their discovery was imminent. They would not have left without me for any other reason. Given the absence of blood and the fact they had time to leave a message, it seemed reasonable to believe they had slipped away before our pursuers arrived. But where had they gone and what did Oracle think I could do to save them? Perhaps that moment hadn't yet arrived. Maybe the awakening of the catalyst would only happen once I found them again.

Someone had torn Tuthmose's house apart, but why? Looking for clues as to where they went? Angry the girls had slipped out of their grasp yet again? Or maybe it wasn't our pursuers who ransacked the house. It might have been someone who noticed the inhabitants were gone and searched for any valuables they had left behind.

If it was Tuthmose who left the message on the windowsill, he probably fled with them. That must be why there were four parallel lines rather than just three. Four lines, four people. If he was with them, I had to believe he would do what he could to keep them safe. I couldn't imagine why he might have gone with them, though. Guilt about his wife, who he had admitted he never loved? A desire to protect the girls because he couldn't protect his son? A sense of responsibility because Hennie and the girls were living in his home?

I didn't need to ask for directions. The wharf would be on the water, so I simply walked along the shoreline until I reached it. I had no supplies, but it was only a day's walk and I didn't want to waste time on foraging. By early afternoon, my stomach was grumbling. I had gotten too used to regular meals.

I expected the wharf to look much like where the boats docked at the palace at Akhetaten, with the twin jetties that stretched out over the Great River. There, the boats would draw up to the jetties and their owners would unload their cargo. This was nothing like that. The ships waiting here were far larger than the boats that sailed the Great River. Massive things with curved prows and multiple sails. Some had human-like figures extending from their prows. Goddesses, perhaps. Protector deities. If we used to have thousands of gods, there must be at least one who protected sea travellers. I wished I knew who. The ships were too big to pull in at the wharf and instead they anchored a little way offshore. Smaller boats transported people and goods between the ships and the wharf.

I showed the bark on which I had copied the images to people at the wharf, and it didn't take long to find someone who knew what the first one meant. He was a sailor, as best I could tell, or at least he had the same look as Tuthmose, who I had thought was a farmer. He studied the images for only a moment before he nodded.

"I think that is Suakin," he said.

"Where is that?" I asked.

He turned and pointed out across the water.

"East," he said. "On the other side of the Red Sea."

"What makes you think it means Suakin?"

"This is the canal." He pointed to the straight line. "That is where a ship approaches. Then you enter the harbour." He traced the space between the two circles with his calloused finger, then tapped the central circle. "That there is Suakin. The larger circle is the mainland across the water."

There was only one ship leaving for Suakin and it would depart at dawn in two days. It was a hive of activity with men loading the transport boats with crates to be ferried out to the ship. I glimpsed fabric poking out from beneath the lid of one. A merchant ship, perhaps. If they sailed with valuable cargo, the captain would employ guards to travel with them. He would not risk his cargo being stolen by pirates. This would be a good ship to travel on.

"Excuse me," I said to a passing man. "Can you tell me where I would find the captain of this ship?"

He looked me up and down. He looked to be Egyptian born, although the angle of his eyes and the shape of his nose suggested one of his parents originated from elsewhere.

"Over there." He gestured with a jerk of his head. "But if you intend to ask for transport, I wouldn't bother. He doesn't like women on board his ship."

He left before I could respond.

I went to stand near the captain and waited until he finished with the man he was speaking to. It hadn't occurred to me I might have trouble getting onboard. I had intended to offer a gem as payment for my transport and had assumed any captain would be pleased to take such a thing in exchange for transporting a single person. It wasn't like I would take up much space.

The man talking with the captain left, and I approached.

"Excuse me," I said.

The captain didn't even look at me, too busy with watching his men load the crates. It was noisy here and perhaps he hadn't heard me. I moved to stand directly in front of him.

"Excuse me," I said a little louder.

His gaze flickered over me and he frowned, already looking annoyed even though I had hardly spoken.

"What do you want?" he asked curtly.

"I hoped to purchase transport on your ship. I need to go to Suakin."

He looked away, apparently finding me uninteresting.

"Send your husband to speak with me," he said.

"I speak for myself."

He glanced at me again and frowned, harder this time.

"Not with me. I don't do business with women. Either send me your husband or go away. I am busy."

"I can pay." I retrieved from my pouch the gem I had intended to offer. It was a pretty sphere of lapis lazuli, polished to a high sheen. I held it out to him. He didn't even look at it before he turned his back on me.

"I have given you my answer," he said.

I gaped at him, then marched around to position myself in front of him again.

"I do not need a husband to speak for me," I said. "I conduct my own business and, as I have told you, I can pay for my transport."

"Woman." He finally looked at me again, although he didn't so much as glance at the gem I held out to him. "Remove yourself from my presence, or I will send for the police to remove you."

"I have done nothing wrong. I am permitted to be here as much as you are."

His gaze filled with distaste, and he turned his head to spit on the ground.

"Where I come from, respectable women stay in their homes. You should not be wandering the streets unaccompanied. I do not need a harlot onboard my ship to distract my men."

He strode away before I could find a response.

I swallowed down the angry reply I wanted to shout after him and shoved the gem back in my pouch. It wasn't the first time I had been called a harlot for daring to speak for myself, and I doubted it would be the last. But it was clear I wouldn't convince him to let me board his ship.

I sat in the shade while I considered my options. He wouldn't negotiate with me and there was likely nothing I could do to change his mind. Maybe I could stow away. Wait until the sailors were all gone for the night. Steal one of the transport boats and row out to the ship. Sneak onboard and find somewhere to hide. Once we were at sea, the captain wouldn't be inclined to return just to bring a woman back to shore.

But although I waited at the wharf until the sailors had gone and everything was quiet, there were still men on his ship. He had indeed hired guards and it seemed they intended to keep watch all night. Stowing away would not be an option. I needed a husband. Or a man willing to pretend to be my husband long enough to sail with me to Crete.

THIRTY-NINE

SETI

Tuthmose said we had to leave because there were soldiers looking for us in the village. He heard them asking if anyone had seen two girls with a young woman and an old woman. Stolen from their family, the men were saying, by a woman who was very sick in the head and thought they were her own children. Their family were desperate to find them and had offered a very large reward. Before we left Grandmother's house in Nubet, she said the bad men would want to find her as well, since they knew she had been looking after us. I hadn't really believed her then.

"They will not be far behind us," Tuthmose said. "Their story sounds genuine and when folk hear of a reward, they will be happy to tell what they know."

"We can go to the oracle," Grandmother said. "Tentamun will know what to do."

"You don't understand," he said. "This is not just one squad. There are many men here. Enough to be in multiple locations at once. We cannot risk going anywhere you have been before. Someone might have seen you going to the oracle. Maybe someone heard Tentamun asking for directions, or has seen her at the oracle's cave. That place is not safe for you."

"We need to get to Tentamun," Grandmother said. "She will keep us safe."

"Hennie, there are too many men," Tuthmose said. "No matter what Tentamun can do, she cannot protect you against that many. We must flee."

"But where do we go?" Grandmother asked. "How will Tentamun find us?"

"Pack some things," he said. "Quickly. Just whatever you can carry easily. There is no time for more than that. I will think of a way to leave a message for her."

"Hurry, girls," Grandmother said. "Grab your clothes and your bed mat and put them in a pack. Put on your sandals. Get your shawl."

"Blankets," Tuthmose said. "Hennie, get some food together. I have an idea about how to leave Tentamun a message."

In not very much time, we were ready to leave. It made me think about the morning we left the palace, although that was a long time ago and I didn't remember it very well. I had been sleepy and didn't want to get out of bed and the sun wasn't even up yet. But Ankhesenpaaten told us to get dressed and get a shawl. I didn't want to, so her captain carried me away in my nightgown. I shoved my feet in my sandals. I wasn't leaving without shoes again.

Nef was ready before me and already waited beside the door. Her face was very white and her lips trembled a little. I stood next to her, clutching my pack, while Hennie shoved food into a basket. Tuthmose was drawing on the windowsill.

"Ready?" he asked, glancing over at us.

Nef's cold fingers found mine and she clutched my hand.

"Tey will find us," I whispered. "You know she will."

FORTY
TEY

I could do nothing about finding a man to pretend to be my husband until morning when the wharf again filled with people. There were men of various nationalities, many of whom were obviously sailors or guards. Others seemed to be couriers or farmers. Surely there must be one here who would pretend to be my husband for a few weeks.

I studied the men, looking for a likely candidate, and disregarded anyone who had the stocky build and dark-hair of the captain. Wherever he was from, it was likely his fellow countrymen shared his views about unaccompanied women.

I spotted a fellow going from captain to captain. Each shook his head at whatever the fellow said and he would slink away, only to approach the next. He had a slight build and looked as if a strong ocean breeze would send him tumbling to his feet. Long arms and legs, large feet he tripped over now and then. He was looking for work, perhaps, but no captain was interested in a man who looked as delicate as he. I sidled up behind him, trying to listen as he approached the last captain.

He was indeed looking for work. He had a sick wife, it seemed, and a newborn, and he would do any work the captain desired. As the others had, the captain waved him away, and the man slunk off. He stood with his shoulders slumped, his arms wrapped around himself, and looked thoroughly dejected.

I wandered over to stand beside him. He paid me no notice. I cleared my throat, wondering how to introduce myself.

"Are you seeking work?" I asked at last.

He started a little and glanced over. The hope faded from his face.

"I am," he said. "And I am too busy to stand here and chatter."

"I have a job for you," I said.

I slipped my fingers into my pouch, searching for the other gem I had set aside in case I needed to offer the captain two jewels to transport me. It was a sapphire, only tiny, but it sparkled in the sun.

"I need to get to Suakin," I said, showing him the gem. "There is a ship sailing tomorrow, but the captain won't speak with me. He said I should send my husband to talk to him. But I have no husband and I am not inclined to find myself one."

He glanced from the gem to me and shrugged.

"I do not know what you think I can do about it," he said.

"I need someone to pretend to be my husband. Arrange transport for both of us with the captain, travel with me to Suakin. Then you would be free to do as you wish."

He glanced down at the gem again.

"And you offer that in payment?" he asked. "How do I know it is not stolen?"

"It was an inheritance," I said. "Pretend to be my husband long enough for me to get to Suakin and it is yours."

He studied the gem again, considering.

"A jewel like this could change your life," I said. "I heard you tell the captain you had a sick wife and a newborn son. This would let you provide for them for a long time if you trade it wisely."

He looked into my eyes as if trying to assess my intent.

"All I have to do is pretend to be your husband until we reach Suakin?" he asked.

"There will be no further obligation of you past that. I need to get there as soon as possible and I must be on the ship that departs tomorrow morning."

He studied the gem again.

"And you will pay for both your passage and mine, I assume?"

I retrieved the lapis lazuli from my pouch and held it up for his inspection.

"So I go to the captain, give him the jewel, and arrange for us both to travel to Suakin," he said. "Then I go on the ship with you and pretend to be your husband. When we reach Suakin, you will give me the sapphire and I can go wherever I want."

A surge of dislike filled me. He intended to use this as an opportunity to leave his wife and child. I swallowed it down before I could say anything I might regret. It was nothing to do with me what he did after we reached Suakin. I had no responsibility towards his family. I nodded, not trusting myself to speak.

"Fine then," he said. "Give me the jewel and I will go speak with the captain. You had better tell me your name. It will not look good if I do not know my 'wife's' name."

"Tentamun," I said.

"I am Ahmes."

He went to the captain and although the man dismissed him at first, clearly having remembered him asking for work, he soon listened more carefully. They talked for a few minutes before Ahmes handed over the gem. He returned to me, looking reasonably cheerful.

"It is done," he said. "The fellow says to be ready to board an hour before dawn."

"I will spend the night here," I said. "Make sure you are back in time. If you aren't on that ship with me tomorrow, you don't get paid."

"You don't intend to go home for the night?"

"I don't live here and I know nobody I could request accommodation of. I have my cloak and I will be warm enough."

"It is not respectable," he said. "A woman alone. You cannot spend the night at the wharf. There isn't even any shelter."

"I did it last night and I can do it again."

He gave a heavy sigh. "You had better come home with me. You can stay the night with my wife and I."

He led me to a cottage that was in even worse condition than Hennie's was when we first arrived. She, at least, had the excuse of poor eyesight and an inability to mend the thatch or mud bricks herself. I wondered what Ahmes' excuse was. The cottage comprised only a single chamber with a bench along one wall holding a couple of storage baskets, a thin blanket folded with little care to neatness, and a low sleeping platform with two bed mats.

His wife, Ini, was a thin, pale woman who hunched into herself as if trying to make herself invisible. She seemed too worn down to show any surprise at her husband bringing home a stranger, but only set the babe down on a rug and began very slowly to prepare a meal. I offered to help, but she waved me away. She paused to cough, a deep wracking noise that must have hurt.

Ahmes and I sat on the rug, the swaddled babe between us. I couldn't see any more of the babe than his pale face. His eyes were closed and his mouth open as he gasped for breath. I didn't have enough experience with babes to know whether this was what he should look like.

"How old is the babe?" I asked.

"Six months." Ahmes glanced at the babe when he whimpered, but made no attempt to pick him up or soothe him. "Ini, how much longer?"

"Almost ready," she said, in a voice that was little more than a whisper. She grasped the bench for support as she coughed.

The babe whimpered again and Ahmes ignored him.

"What is his name?" I felt like I should try to make conversation, even though Ahmes seemed content to sit there and ignore me.

"Ahmes," he said. "The first-born male in my family is always called Ahmes."

I nodded, not knowing what else to say.

Ini came bearing a tray of bread and sliced cucumber, which she set down between us. She left and slowly returned with mugs of beer. Ahmes was already filling his belly before she even sat down.

There was no conversation as we ate. I couldn't think of what to say, and neither Ahmes nor Ini seemed inclined to talk. It wasn't until Ahmes had eaten his fill that he spoke again.

"I have got work," he said.

Ini only nodded and took another bite of her bread.

"I will be gone for a few weeks," Ahmes said.

I waited for him to explain, but he didn't tell her what he was doing or that we travelled to Suakin together or that it was me who would pay him. Ini showed no curiosity.

After our meal, Ahmes showed me where I could sleep. I had neither bed mat nor blanket, having left mine at Oracle's cave, and he offered me nothing. I covered myself with my cloak and tried to sleep, but the babe was restless, whimpering often, although he never cried. Maybe the poor thing didn't have the strength for it. Ini held him and although she tried to soothe him, she didn't speak to him. Perhaps she knew he would soon depart for the West. After all, many babes didn't survive their first year. Maybe she was trying not to get too attached to him.

Ahmes put together a pack of things he would take with him and then lay on his mat. Ini was still trying to calm the babe.

"Can you not keep him quiet?" Ahmes grumbled. "I have to work tomorrow. And if you are going to sit up with him all night, at least put out the lamp."

Ini shut off the light without replying. Baby Ahmes continued to whimper, but I eventually fell asleep.

When I woke, the chamber was dark. I held myself very still, wondering what had woken me. Something nearby moved. Somebody breathed, far too close to me. I slid a dagger from its sheath.

A hand groped at my waist. I grabbed it.

He stilled.

"What do you think you are doing?" I asked.

"Just wanted to see the jewel again." Ahmes voice was sulky. "You barely let me inspect it before."

"So you thought to relieve me of it while I slept?"

"I just wanted to look at it."

I touched the blade of my dagger to his hand.

"Let's get something straight, Ahmes. I don't like being woken in the night with a man pawing at my body."

"I was hardly—"

"If you touch me again, I will take your hand off at the wrist. If you have trouble getting work now, imagine how much harder it will be if you only have one hand."

He moved away from me.

"No need to be hasty," he said. "You are overreacting."

I took a deep breath, trying to calm myself before I responded. As much as I disliked him, I needed him. For now, at least. I couldn't get to Suakin without him.

"Get some sleep," I said. "I want to be at the boat well before dawn."

FORTY-ONE

TEY

I slept restlessly after that, not wanting to give Ahmes another chance to relieve me of my pouch. When I judged it was less than two hours before dawn, I rose and rolled up my mat. I didn't try to be quiet and by the time I finished, Ahmes was stirring. The babe whimpered and I regretted having woken him. He and Ini probably got little enough sleep as it was.

After wrestling with my conscience overnight, I had come to a decision. I had little doubt that Ahmes didn't intend to return home once I gave him the sapphire. As bad a husband as he might be, Ini probably had no other options and no way of supporting herself without him. I went to baby Ahmes and pretended to farewell him while I tucked a finger ring set with a large yellow gem beneath him. Ini would find it as soon as she picked up the babe and hopefully that wouldn't be until after Ahmes and I had left. I doubted Ahmes himself would bother to hold the babe before then.

I slipped outside to give them some privacy for their farewells. However, Ahmes followed me out almost immediately. Their farewell must have been brief indeed. I waited for him to offer some explanation about what had happened overnight, but he said nothing.

The captain didn't even look at me as we boarded. He spoke briefly to Ahmes, telling him we should go below deck until we set sail and stay out of the crew's way at all times.

Below the deck smelled of unwashed bodies. I didn't wait for Ahmes to tell me where to sit and instead settled with my back to the bulkhead and where I could see out through the hatch. Not that there was much of a view from here — just a patch of dark sky. Every now and then, one of the crew walked past, obscuring my view of the sky for a few moments. A man brought a couple of crates down below, stacking them neatly beside the others. At last, the ship's timber groaned and we were on our way.

I kept to myself while we sailed and tried to forget Ahmes was with me. I found myself disliking him more every time we spoke. I kept remembering how he rebuked Ini for taking too long to settle the babe, and that he hadn't told her he was leaving Egypt. Unless he told her in those brief moments before he followed me outside, she didn't know where he had gone.

Theirs seemed a strange relationship, but perhaps this was what marriage was like for most women. I thanked Aten that Papa had never pushed me to take a husband, and I felt a deep sense of satisfaction at having left the finger ring for Ini. Maybe I was wrong about Ahmes and he did intend to go home, but I doubted his wife would be there waiting for him if he did.

Our journey was tedious with day after day of clear weather and fine seas. At first I trained on the deck, both to keep myself fit and to pass the time. But the crew were clearly unused to a woman doing such activities and paid me too much attention. After whistles and stares and more than one lewd comment, I retreated down below. I was used to men staring when I trained, but the soldiers of Akhetaten were more respectful than these sailors. It was less pleasant to train in the half-dark and the stink, but at least there was nobody to stare or comment.

When I wasn't training, I went back up top to watch our progress. I tried to stay out of the crew's way, but even when I did nothing but look out at the water, they still leered. I did my best to ignore them. Aten damn them, but I didn't intend to spend the entire journey trapped below deck.

I tried not to worry about Hennie and the girls, but there was little else to occupy my mind with. Were they safe or had our pursuers caught up to them again? Had the girls been taken back to Akhetaten? Perhaps they were all long gone to the West by now. My task might be over — failed — and I never even knew.

What would I do if I learned they were all dead? I wasn't sure I would go back to Akhetaten. How could I look Papa in the eyes and admit I failed to keep them safe? How would I face Intef? If their sister, the queen, had been killed to make way for Nef or Seti to take the throne, he would never forgive me. But if the queen was dead, Intef had probably gone to the West ahead of her. And Papa would know it was all my fault.

I fiddled with my mother's ring, twisting it around my finger, and wished I had someone to share my fears with. Tuthmose's face popped into my mind and I pushed his image away. How could I think such a thing at a time like this? That he was an attractive man who seemed interested in me and was kind to Hennie and the girls didn't change the fact that I had no desire for a husband. I didn't need someone to tell me what I was permitted to do and when I could do it. I would make my own way in the world, just as I always had.

I saw little of Ahmes as we sailed and I wasn't interested enough to find out how he spent his time. When we encountered each other, we spoke only if necessary, although I often saw him eyeing my pouch. I wondered how long it would take Ini to decide to leave.

A couple of weeks later, we reached Suakin, and I understood why the man who interpreted Tuthmose's drawing had thought it depicted the harbour here. We did indeed sail along a canal, which emptied into a circular harbour. Suakin was an island in the centre. The message would be obvious to anyone who had been here.

How did Oracle know the design on her blanket would be

meaningful for me? I now wondered whether she really needed the threads for something else or whether she made me spend all those hours unpicking it just so I would remember the design and know it was important when I saw it again. It was a mystery and I would have liked to ask her about it. I doubted she would explain herself, though, and she had said she rarely understood the wisdom she received. She may have known no more than that the image would be significant to me.

We reached the wharf and disembarked from the ship. As soon as his feet touched the wooden planks, Ahmes held out his hand.

"You can pay me now and I will be on my way," he said.

I withdrew the gem from my pouch and passed it to him without comment. I would be glad to be rid of him.

Ahmes took the gem and held it up to the light.

"Are you sure it is a genuine sapphire?" he asked.

"It is a bit late to be wondering."

He frowned at the gem.

"Now that I look at it properly, I see it is not as fine as I thought. What else can you give me?"

"That is the payment we agreed." My tone was curter now. Did he think to con me?

"I doubt it is real. It looks like polished glass to me."

"You are an expert in gems now, are you?"

"Show me what else you have in there." He gestured towards my pouch. "You must have something of more value you can offer for the considerable time and effort I have expended in escorting you so far."

"What effort? You have spent your days lazing on the deck and staring at the sea. That is the payment we agreed on and you will get nothing further."

He snatched at my wrist.

"Show me the pouch."

It took hardly any effort to pull myself out of his grasp.

"I suggest you keep your hands to yourself," I said.

I was tempted to pull a dagger on him, but didn't want to

cause a commotion and risk getting myself arrested before I found Hennie and the girls.

"You have tricked me," he said. "You promised me a sapphire, but it is just a piece of glass."

"I assure you it is genuine." I couldn't imagine a gem from the queen's collection would be anything less. "Besides, you inspected it before we left. You were satisfied with it then. Interesting you now claim it is worthless."

"If you do not give me something better, I will go to the police."

I shrugged. "Go ahead. Show them your sapphire and tell them you don't feel you received adequate compensation for spending a couple of weeks lazing around. You will probably find the gem confiscated as 'evidence' and you will never see it again. Then you will have nothing. So I advise you to take it and leave."

"You have more than that. You can give me something better."

I turned my back on him and walked away

"Give me more," he called after me.

I half expected him to follow me, but it seemed he wasn't that determined. Likely he knew the sapphire was real, but thought to cheat something else out of me while he could. I hoped he did decide to go home so he would know that Ini had left. Wherever she went, she and Baby Ahmes would be better off without him.

FORTY-TWO

TEY

The day was late and as much as I longed to start my search, accommodation needed to be my priority.

The Suakin harbour was a bustling area. Folk of many nationalities pushed their way through the crowds. I couldn't identify where most of them were from. There were a few Egyptians and some Kushites, but the others were a mystery to me. Their languages mingled in the air, some soft melodic tones, others harsh and guttural. I finally comprehended I was in a foreign country for the first time and likely wouldn't be able to communicate with most of the people here. I needed to find someone who spoke either Egyptian or the language of the Sand Wanderers.

I approached a couple of Egyptian men, but they were busy and not interested in stopping to talk with an unknown woman. At last I spotted an old man who had the appearance of my homeland sitting with his back to the trunk of a shady dom palm. He seemed to do nothing other than watch the crowd. I went to sit beside him.

"Good day to you," I said.

After how quickly the other men had pushed past me, I half expected him to get up and walk away. He grunted at me, but didn't seem inclined to leave, so I sat beside him.

"I have only just arrived," I said. "Do you know where I can find accommodation? Perhaps a woman willing to take in a tenant for a few days for work around the house? I can do any repairs that are needed or work in the garden."

He kept his face towards the crowd, although I was sure he inspected me out of the corner of his eye.

"I might know someone," he said. "My daughter could do with some help. Her husband is a sailor and is rarely at home. When he is, he is not inclined to do much, preferring to rest until he goes back out to sea again. She might give you somewhere to sleep in exchange for some chores."

"I would be grateful if you could give me directions to her home," I said.

I wanted to ask if he had seen anyone matching the description of Hennie and the girls, but bit my tongue. Once I had secured accommodation would be soon enough to look for them. Since he seemed inclined to help me at the moment, I didn't want to change his mind by asking questions he thought might bring trouble to his daughter's household.

The old man's name was Nakht and his daughter was Meresamun. I knocked on the door of her home and it was opened by a young girl who bore a clear resemblance to Nakht. This must be his granddaughter. Another girl peered over the shoulder of the first. There was more than one granddaughter, then.

"Is your mother home?" I asked.

"Mama," one of the girls called. "Someone at the door."

"What have I told you about opening the door to strangers?"

Meresamun was a rather harried looking woman. A headscarf held her dark hair back from her face and she wore a long, loose gown in the style that seemed to be favoured by the women here. I saw several others dressed like this at the harbour. She carried a babe on her hip, bouncing the girl as she studied me.

"Are you Meresamun?" I asked. "Nakht sent me. I am seeking a few days of accommodation and he thought you might allow me to stay in exchange for some work around your home."

Meresamun looked me up and down. Her face was carefully blank, and I got no sense of what she thought of me turning up on her doorstep.

"One night," she said at last. "I will see whether you are any use before I decide whether to let you stay longer."

She indicated with a jerk of her head for me to enter. Once my eyes adjusted to the dimness inside, I found the house comprised two chambers. This one was scattered with toys and was clearly where the children spent most of their time. Two girls — younger than the ones who had answered the door — played in the corner with wooden blocks. So there were at least five daughters and none of them old enough to be much help.

"I will be out of your way during the mornings," I said. "When I return in the afternoon, I can do whatever you need. Mend the roof, fix shelves or shutters, dig your vegetable garden. Just tell me what needs doing."

The babe cried. Meresamun sat on the rug and put the babe to her breast.

"The vegetable garden has not been weeded for a few months," she said. "My husband was supposed to do it last time he was home. I am too busy with the children to do such a thing and well he knows it."

"I can go do that now."

I itched to start my search, but she had said she would judge me today. Besides, the morning was already gone. She wouldn't be pleased if I said I wouldn't do anything until tomorrow afternoon, but still expected to spend the night under her roof.

Meresamun nodded and her attention turned now to one of the other girls who had tripped and came, crying, to show her a bloodied knee. I slipped out the door, thankful to be away from the children. At least Nef and Seti were old enough to not cry over a scraped knee.

The garden looked like it had been a lot longer than a few months since it was touched. It was overgrown and I didn't recognise some of the plants. Since this was a foreign country, she might have vegetables planted here that I hadn't seen before, and I hoped I wasn't pulling out anything that was useful to her. It took a good part of the afternoon to clear the weeds, then I dug another couple of cubits using a pitchfork I found leaning against the back wall of the house. The ground was dry and I was sweating by the time I finished. I headed back into the house.

"Do you have any vegetable seeds?" I asked Meresamun. "I have weeded the garden and cleared a bit more. If you have seeds, I can plant them out for you."

She gave me a bemused look, clearly surprised to find I had managed to weed the garden. Perhaps it had been a test.

"No seeds," she said. "But I need to go to the market tomorrow morning. I can pick some up."

"I will plant them in the afternoon then," I said. "What else do you need doing?"

She listed a few other chores, all minor things, like a shutter that didn't hang right, and I completed them before sundown.

"You surprise me, Tentamun," Meresamun said as we ate our evening meal, she and her daughters and I sitting in a circle on the rug. "How does a woman learn to do such things as fix a broken shutter?"

"My husband taught me. He went to the West a couple of years ago and I have been used to doing things for myself since then."

"My husband is at sea. He doesn't come home often and when he does, he is about as useful as a dead husband."

"Nakht mentioned he isn't here often." I needed to change the subject. If the conversation was to be a comparison of our spouses, it would be too easy to say the wrong thing since I knew little of husbands, only what Hennie had told me and what I observed of Ahmes. "How is it that your family lives here? You have the appearance of an Egyptian woman."

"My father was a sailor in his younger years. My mother died when I was maybe five years old or so, and my father met a woman when his ship came to Suakin at some point. He decided to come here to be with her, so he went back to Egypt to fetch me. We had a neighbour who cared for me when he was at sea. By the time he came back, the woman had married someone else, but my father didn't have the heart to go home again. So we stayed."

She shrugged as if to say it was all the same to her. I supposed it probably was. She had been too young when she left to have much memory of her homeland.

I asked about her daughters and she gave their names and ages, although I forgot all of them except the oldest, Pyhia, who was seven. The same age as Seti when we first met. Pyhia studied me with large, brown eyes and seemed much older than her years. Or perhaps Seti had been young for that age. I didn't have enough experience with children to know.

"Do you go to school?" I asked her, although I immediately regretted it. Perhaps only the girls of wealthy families attended school here, just as in Egypt.

"No," Pyhia said after a cautious glance at her mother, as if wondering whether she might say the wrong thing.

"I am usually too busy to think about getting her to school." Meresamun sounded embarrassed and her cheeks looked red in the lamplight. "There are too many children underfoot to spend time in sending just one to school."

"I would like to learn how to read," Pyhia said. "But Mama says girls don't need to know that."

"That is right," Meresamun said. "When you are old enough, you will marry and bring up a brood of children, just like your mama. There is no need for reading when you are busy chasing after children all day. We will just have to see that your husband has a more useful career than sailing. Farming perhaps. That is a good occupation and will always mean food on the table. You, my child, will not spend your life waiting for a sailor to bring home his pay so you can go buy food at the market."

I didn't quite know what to say. Pyhia's childhood was very different from mine. Papa had encouraged me to learn all I could, even though as a girl I was not expected to learn much, and he had been happy to spend his evenings teaching me to read and do sums.

By Pyhia's age, Papa had already taught me to defend myself and gave me my own dagger, which I carried everywhere, tucked into the waistband of my skirt. He expected me to make myself useful, even as a child. I was not permitted to sit inside and play with toys all day as Meresamun's daughters seemed to do. Papa paid a woman to bake bread and brew beer for us, but I was expected to sweep the floor and keep the house tidy. I weeded the vegetable garden and fetched water and made sure Intef didn't get himself into too much trouble. Pyhia was hardly the only child to grow up without her father present, but was this what life was like for other children? Playing games all day and fighting for attention from an overworked mother?

Although I had always said I had no intention of marrying or having babes, I realised now I hadn't understood what that life would be like, other than the obvious of cleaning and cooking and minding the children. I had never considered the bone-weariness of caring for multiple children with an absent father. The lack of sleep when the babe fussed all night and there was nobody but yourself to look after her. The constant cacophony of children playing and chattering, shrieking and fighting. The inability to do so much as relieve yourself without at least one child clinging to your skirt. Thank Aten Papa had never forced that life on me.

My feelings towards Nef and Seti had changed during the time I spent with Oracle, although I only just realised it now. Before, I had been wrapped in my bitterness and resentment at finding myself responsible for two young girls. But having been separated from them for almost seven months now, my feelings had softened. Nef tried hard to be useful and with distance from Seti, I finally understood why Hennie said we were so alike.

After spending an evening with Meresamun's daughters, I realised how different Nef and Seti were. They played together like Meresamun's girls, and they bickered from time to time, but they didn't constantly shriek and giggle. Maybe it was because there were only two of them, or maybe their life had taught them to be more serious. Perhaps they knew more of the perilousness of life than Meresamun's daughters did.

I was finally able to resume my search the following day. I spent the morning asking anyone I could find who spoke Egyptian whether they had seen two girls arrive a few months ago with their grandmother and possibly their father. It was such an unremarkable description that I hardly expected anyone to recall such a thing. It must be a commonplace event for families to step off the ships, come in search of a new life, or to spend time with elderly grandparents. Nobody would remember unless I could give something more specific, even though I described Hennie as best I could. I even asked whether there had been soldiers looking for two girls and an old woman, but that only rewarded me with sideways glances and quick excuses to leave.

There were frustratingly few Egyptians here and far more people who I couldn't communicate with. If only I could speak the local language. Someone must have seen something.

FORTY-THREE
TEY

When the sun reached its peak, I returned to Meresamun's house, feeling dispirited. She didn't ask where I had been, only listed several chores she needed done. I fixed the leg on a stool — the only one she had — and patched a hole near the window where the wind whistled in. I planted the vegetable seeds Meresamun bought at the market and fetched half a dozen buckets of water for her. The chores were a welcome distraction, and I tried to keep my mind on them rather than worrying about how I would find Hennie and the girls without speaking the local language.

Meresamun was a little friendlier that evening and even smiled at me as I helped carry the food from her workbench to the rug. We sat, surrounded by her daughters, and I served myself a portion of the meal she had prepared, which was a watery soup that seemed to have a tiny amount of fish. From the anxious looks Meresamun gave me, I suspected she must have gone to some effort with it. The girls chattered — some nonsense about something that had happened today which I couldn't quite understand — and the babe fussed.

"Tentamun, I don't think you have told me why you are here," Meresamun said after she had settled the babe on her breast. It seemed to be the only time the babe was quiet.

I hesitated. I could hardly say I was searching for my daughters, as her next question would be how I came to be separated from them.

"I am looking for my brother," I said and hoped I hadn't already spent long enough thinking to make her suspicious. "He came here about six months ago, with his daughters and our mother. I have not heard from him since, so I have come to see whether they are well."

"I see." Meresamun held her feeding babe with one hand and spooned soup into her own mouth with the other. "Why did they come to Suakin?"

"I don't know. He never told me."

"And his wife, where is she?"

"Gone to the West," I said.

"A fresh start perhaps, then. Did he love her?"

"I suppose so. I cannot say I ever asked."

"How old are his daughters?"

"Nine and ten, or thereabouts."

"Old enough to be useful then." Meresamun shot a look at Pyhia. "And I suppose with no mother, they have had to grow up faster than other girls."

"I cared for them as best I could over the last couple of years."

It was only after I spoke that I realised how defensive my tone was. Meresamun gave no sign she had noticed.

"Do you miss them?" she asked. "Or has it been a relief to not have extra children to care for?"

"Extra children?"

"In addition to your own. I suppose you do have children of your own?"

"No. It.. Uh, never happened for us."

Of course, she would assume I had children since I had mentioned a husband. Somehow I didn't think Meresamun would be the kind of woman who would understand if I said I didn't want her life. As much as she might moan about her absent husband and the constant children underfoot, she had probably never imagined any other life for herself. It was me who was different. Me who wanted something different from what other women wanted. Normal women.

"Well, you are not that old," she said. "There is still time for you to marry again and bear children. Best get to it as soon as possible. You are not getting younger and let me tell you, you feel it more with every babe. These old bones of mine are certainly tired these days."

I studied her face, wondering how old she was. If she had married at thirteen and birthed Pyhia a year later, she might be as young as twenty-one, only a year older than me. I studied the circle of daughters with new eyes. At my age, Meresamun probably already had four children.

"I suppose I have been busy with my brother's children," I muttered. "There hasn't really been time for anything else."

"And yet you chose not to come with them when they moved here? I would think that after mothering them for so long, you must love them as your own. How could you bear to let them go without you, especially with your husband dead?"

She truly saw no alternative version of her life. No variation in which she wasn't the mother of several children. The wife of an absent husband.

"My brother thought to marry again once they were settled," I said. "I knew it would be easier for him to find a new wife without me around. Few women would want to take on their new husband's sister in addition to his children."

The babe started to fuss again and Meresamun rose. She paced the chamber, patting the babe on the back.

"I am not sure I could bear to give them up," she said eventually. "They would be like my own daughters and I could never give any of them up, as much as they exhaust me and try my patience."

How many times had I regretted taking responsibility for the girls, or Seti at any rate? Surely after more than two years together, I should have grown to love them at least a little? I looked around the circle of girls again. Two squabbled over the last of the soup. The middle child — I couldn't remember her name — had a dreamy look on her face and seemed lost in her own thoughts. The younger had drawn her knees up to her chest and rested her chin on them, seemingly almost asleep. The babe had settled at last. This could have been my life.

A feeling of confinement welled within me, sudden and overwhelming. I needed to get out of here.

"I will fetch some water," I said.

I grabbed a bucket and hurried out of the cottage. I took my time getting the water and when I returned, Meresamun and her daughters had gone to bed. As I waited for sleep, I planned tomorrow's search.

But by the time dawn came, the babe had fallen ill.

FORTY-FOUR

TEY

Meresamun seemed unconcerned as she wiped the babe with a cloth dipped in water even while she tried to get her to feed. Sweat dripped down the babe's face and she kept turning her head away from her mother's breast. This was nothing like whatever baby Ahmes had suffered from. For the first time, I realised how fortunate I was that nothing more than the mildest of illness had afflicted either Nef or Seti in the time they had been in my care.

"Should I find a healer?" I asked.

"It is just a childhood fever. They all get them from time to time. She will recover in a day or two."

"Do you need me to mind the other girls while you look after her?"

I didn't want to spend time away from my search, especially since I had agreed to complete her chores in the afternoons, but I couldn't leave her like this. To my relief, Meresamun shook her head.

"This happens all the time," she said. "Go. Look for your brother. She will probably be much better by the time you return."

But when I came back in the middle of the day, the babe was visibly sicker, even to my inexperienced eye. This morning she was flushed and squirming, but now she was pale and still. It reminded me of Nef after she was dosed with what we suspected was too much poppy.

"Perhaps I should go for the healer?" I suggested.

"No, no, I am sure she is almost through the worst of it. This stage won't last long and then she will recover."

I shepherded her older daughters out of the house, leaving Meresamun with just the babe. The girls were happy enough to play outside and when they tired of that, I took them for a long walk. I had never had to entertain Nef and Seti, so I didn't know what else to do with them, but if I could wear them out, perhaps they would be quiet this evening. Meresamun would surely be exhausted after caring for a sick child all day. By the time we returned, the babe was sweating again and Meresamun's forehead creased with worry.

"I think you should go for the healer," she said. "Although she will have to wait for her payment until my husband bothers to come home again."

She gave me directions and I hurried off. The healer was a wizened old woman who didn't seem concerned when I described the babe's symptoms. She brought a basket filled with little jars and followed me back to Meresamun's. I kept the children in the other chamber while the healer inspected the babe. From the little I could hear, she seemed calm and competent. She didn't speak to me as she left, just slipped out the door and hurried away.

"What did she say?" It was only after I asked that I realised Meresamun was wiping away tears.

She shook her head but didn't look at me.

"Nothing can be done," she said.

Shocked at her words, it took me a few heartbeats to find a reply.

"What do you mean?" I asked at last. "Surely she has a potion or some other remedy that will help. Prayers, spells. When my—" I caught myself, realising I had been about to say my daughter "—

my brother's daughter was ill, the physician gave us herbs to burn and said to lay her favourite flowers on her chest."

"Did she recover?"

From Meresamun's distracted voice, I figured she was only asking to be polite.

"She did. Maybe another healer will have other remedies to offer."

"She is the only one within walking distance." Meresamun smoothed the girl's hair back from her forehead. "This is not the first child I have lost. She has two brothers who died as infants and one who was born without breath."

Meresamun must be older than I thought.

"I will pray to Aten for her," I said.

I didn't know whether she worshipped our Egyptian gods or perhaps one of Suakin, but I supposed it didn't matter. If the gods were willing, they might yet save the child.

But by the next morning Meresamun too had fallen ill. I woke with dawn but lay on the mat she had loaned me, not wanting to disturb her since she had been up most of the night. It was only when I realised she hadn't stirred, even though the children were playing a raucous game that involved a song and much clapping of hands, that I realised something was wrong.

"Meresamun?"

I crouched beside her bed mat and she looked up at me blearily. Her face was flushed and sweating. I fetched some beer and a cloth for her forehead.

"Takhat," she whispered.

I figured that must be the babe.

"I will check on her."

Takhat was deathly pale and didn't stir, even when I shook her shoulder. Her breathing was shallow, and now and then she gave a weak cough.

"She lives," I said to Meresamun.

"Better?" she whispered. "Worse?"

I didn't want to tell her, but it didn't seem right to lie.

"I think she is worse."

Meresamun closed her eyes and didn't speak again.

I fed the other children the last of the bread and wondered whether I should try to buy them some more since I had only the vaguest idea of how to make it myself. I stayed in the cottage that morning and tried to keep the children occupied. The condition of Meresamun and Takhat didn't seem to change. I debated going for the healer again, but wasn't sure I should leave the children and it was too far for the littlest ones to walk.

Frustration welled within me at being delayed again from my search, but I could hardly go now, not with Meresamun being so ill. If only her husband would return, but she had said she never knew when he would come back. If Hennie was here, she might know a way to treat both Meresamun and the babe. One of the Sand Wanderer women had taught her all about medicinal plants. Hennie had wanted me to learn too, but I was always too busy doing other things.

Takhat went to the West around the middle of the day. She breathed shallowly when I checked on her, but when I went back a few minutes later, her chest had stilled. Meresamun seemed delirious, tossing on her bed mat and muttering things that sounded like nonsense. I didn't think she would understand if I told her the babe was gone.

There seemed no choice but to leave the other children now. Something needed to be done with Takhat's body, but would Meresamun want her embalmed in the Egyptian way or something else? She had been in Suakin so long that maybe she would prefer whatever customs the local inhabitants had. We Egyptians believed a person couldn't be resurrected in the afterlife without their body being properly prepared, but perhaps the Kushites knew another way. Perhaps their gods had different demands.

I took the babe and asked around at the wharf until I found someone who could tell me where Nakht lived. He wasn't at home, so I sat by his door with the babe in my lap and waited. A couple of hours passed before he returned and I spent the time trying not to worry that Meresamun had gone to the West while I sat here with her babe's body. Finally, I spotted Nakht approaching the cottage.

"Oh," he said as he realised what I held. He stopped walking and seemed to take a moment to gather himself, then came to crouch in front of me. "Dear child."

"The healer came last night but said nothing could be done. I am sorry to tell you Meresamun is also ill."

Nakht kept his gaze on the babe and sighed heavily. Then he reached to take her from me.

"I will make arrangements," he said.

"Will you come to Meresamun once you are done? She needs someone to care for her and to look after the children."

"I am no good with things like that. I dislike being around sick people. It would be best to leave that to you."

"I cannot. I have things—"

"I know she would appreciate your kindness in bringing the child to me. Go now. I will look after Takhat."

"But—"

He went into his house and closed the door behind him.

Why did he expect me to look after his sick daughter and her children? They were his family, were they not? They were not my responsibility. I knocked on the door, but he didn't answer.

"Nakht," I called. "You need to find someone else to look after Meresamun. I cannot do it."

But he didn't open the door, no matter how hard I knocked. I would have gone right in and confronted him, but he had barred the door.

Not knowing what else to do, I went to the healer. She accompanied me back to Meresamun's home, although she seemed less willing this time on learning the babe had died and Meresamun was ill and still had no way of paying her. She crouched beside Meresamun's bed mat and studied her for only a few moments before saying a quick prayer over her and getting to her feet.

"Is that all you can do?" I asked.

The healer shot a pointed look at the girls and nodded towards the door. I followed her out of the cottage.

"She is not as far gone as the babe," she said. "There is still hope she might recover."

"You must be able to do something for her."

"She is past the point of intervention. It is up to the gods now. She will either recover or she won't."

"But what about the children?" I asked. "Her father will not come to care for them. Does she have other family or perhaps a friend who could look after them?"

"Just keep doing whatever you are doing," she said. "I did not examine them, but they all look well enough. If any of them show signs of fever, send for me again. I may be able to help if I see them early enough."

She patted me on the shoulder.

"You are doing just fine," she said, then hurried away.

I could only stare after her, wondering why everyone expected me to be the one who cared for Meresamun and her children. What choice did I have, though? Meresamun had been kind enough to let me stay in her home and she had nobody else to help her. As much as I longed to resume my search for Hennie and the girls, I felt obliged to stay. I prayed to Aten that Meresamun would recover and quickly.

FORTY-FIVE
TEY

Meresamun lingered between life and death. With each day, my frustration grew at not being able to continue my search, but I couldn't leave her children with nobody to care for them. I slipped away every day to knock on Nakht's door, but he never opened it to me. I was tempted to sit outside his house until he did — he would have to open the door eventually — but I feared leaving the children for too long. What would they do if they were alone in the cottage and discovered their mother dead? At least, none of the others were showing any sign of illness. Not yet anyway.

Pyhia was a great help to me while I cared for her mother. I hadn't expected much of her, but she took charge of the younger girls and did her best to keep them busy. She helped prepare meals, although she didn't know how to cook so once the bread was gone, our diet mostly consisted of such vegetables as could be eaten raw. She even went off to the market by herself and returned with a basket of food and an assurance that she had solemnly promised the farmer her father would pay when he came home next.

After four long days, Meresamun's fever broke. Another day passed before she had the strength to hold a mug on her own and a full week before she seemed well enough that I thought I could resume my search the following morning. But when I woke the next day, I was too weak to get up from my bed mat.

The fever started an hour later.

I had little sense of time as I tossed and turned. There were only times when I sweated and times I didn't. Times when I slept and times I didn't. My dreams were jumbled and confusing, strange montages that were far too bright and made no sense. Every now and then, someone wiped my forehead or held a spoon to my lips. The bed mat beneath me grew soaked with sweat, but I didn't have enough strength to roll over, let alone get up.

I woke to a dark chamber and my mother sitting beside me. Strange that I could see her so clearly, despite the darkness. She leaned over me to stroke my forehead and when I inhaled, I caught the scent of her cinnamon perfume.

"A little longer, dear child," she said to me. "Just a little longer."

When I next woke, the light in the chamber seemed painfully bright. I could barely open my eyes against it, but I could still smell my mother's perfume. Someone wiped a wet cloth over my face. She was still here.

I pried open my eyes, although they teared from the brightness. When I realised it was only Meresamun who attended me, my heart felt like it tore in two. I turned my face away, not wanting her to see my tears. Of course, it couldn't have been my mother, but in my delirium I had believed.

"Do you hear me, Tentamun?" she asked.

She raised my head a little and held something to my mouth. I drank.

"I hear you," I mumbled.

"Ahh. I think the worst has passed then."

"My mother." The words slipped out before I could catch them.

"Yes, you kept saying something about your mother. I couldn't quite make out what it was. You seemed to think I was her."

So it hadn't been my mother after all. I had smelled her perfume though, both during the night and again when I woke. I hadn't realised I remembered her scent until then.

More days passed as I recovered my strength. It seemed I had been iller than Meresamun. At first I couldn't even sit unaided, but a week later I was able to take short walks outside the cottage. Only twenty paces at first, but every day I forced myself to go further than the day before.

By the time I was strong enough to jog a little, I figured more than a month had passed since I fell ill. Another month in which Hennie and the girls might have moved on. Might have left Suakin and gone to Aten-only-knew-where. I prayed I would still be able to follow their trail. They expected me to find them. They wouldn't have left the pictures on Tuthmose's windowsill otherwise.

When I finally left Meresamun's home, her daughters crowded around me, hugging my waist and clutching my hands.

"Don't go," one of them said to me. "You could stay with us."

"Tentamun cannot stay," Meresamun said to her. "We have kept her here long enough. She needs to go find her family now."

I hugged them back and extricated myself from their grasps. Although I had become somewhat fond of them during the weeks I had been here, I was pleased to leave. It had been difficult looking after Meresamun and her daughters, and exhausting, but I left with a new respect for women like her. I had never comprehended the strength a woman must possess to survive such a life, especially if her husband was of no help. And yet this was the life I was supposed to want, with a husband being my prize for accepting that life.

I went straight to Nakht's house. This time, he opened the door to me.

"You owe me a debt," I said. "I looked after your daughter and her children when nobody else did. It should have been her own family who did that."

Nakht at least looked ashamed.

"You seemed to manage," he said. "I judged it best to leave it to you."

"It was not my responsibility. They are not my family, and this has greatly delayed me in finding my brother and his daughters."

"I cannot bear to be near the children when they are sick. They whine and cry and smell odorous. That is a task much better suited to a woman."

"She is your daughter. Your responsibility."

He shrugged at me.

"She is recovered now, is she not? You are free to go about your business?"

"And you are going to help me since I have spent so long looking after your family. I need a person who speaks the local language. You will come help me look for someone who has seen my family."

Nakht looked like he wanted to refuse, but I glared so hard that he sighed.

"Fine, then. Come back tomorrow and we can begin your search."

"No, we are going right now."

I turned and started walking.

"Well, come on," I called to him.

With another sigh, he hurried after me.

FORTY-SIX

TEY

We went to the wharf and I instructed Nakht to ask each of the captains if they had transported a man and his daughters and mother from Egypt a few months ago. But none of the captains had seen them.

"Is there anywhere else in Suakin they could have arrived?" I asked Nakht, but he shook his head.

"All ships dock here. But of course, different ships arrive every day. Some will only be here once every couple of weeks, others once in a few months. It is unlikely the captain you seek will be here on the same day you are asking."

He was right, of course, but I couldn't bear the thought of spending months coming to the harbour every day to see which new ship had arrived and hoping that today would be the one in which I found the captain who transported them. And it was possible the captain wouldn't remember, or didn't know where they were going next, or that he had transported someone else who matched the description I gave. Relying on finding the right captain seemed like a strategy doomed to failure.

"They would have needed transport," I said. "If they didn't settle here in Suakin, maybe they went to the mainland. Let's talk to anyone they might have sought transport from — couriers, farmers, men transporting cargo."

"Over there then." Nakht pointed. "That is where cargo from the ships goes for transport."

There were a dozen men there with carts and oxen. Some were already busy loading their carts; others still waited. We asked each of them, but nobody remembered transporting Hennie and the girls.

"Tomorrow then," I said to Nakht. "Come back in the morning and we will ask the captains who arrive overnight. Someone saw them. Someone knows where they are."

He sighed.

"I cared for your daughter and her children when you wouldn't," I said fiercely. "This is no more than you owe me."

"Fine, then."

He left quickly, perhaps before I could ask anything else of him.

It was only early afternoon, but I didn't know what else to do with myself. I had told Meresamun I wouldn't be back, not wanting to risk being delayed any further. I had nowhere to sleep tonight, but I'd find a spot on the beach if I needed to. There were no new ships in sight, so it was unlikely there would be anyone else to ask today, and without Nakht, I would be lucky to find a captain I could communicate with.

I went to the marketplace to ask around there. It might be pointless, but at least I felt like I was trying to find them. Maybe one of the women who shopped here every day remembered something. Or perhaps one of the old men who sat around the edges had seen them.

The market was busier than I expected. Perhaps because so many ships had recently arrived and new goods were available. I pushed my way through the crowd, wondering where to start.

Then I saw dark hair. The glimpse of a face as the girl turned away.

"Nef?" I called.

I pushed through the crowd.

"Nef, wait."

She was in a hurry. No matter how quickly I went, she was always a little ahead of me, slipping through gaps that were too small for me. I shoved my way past a pair of chattering women. Elbowed an old man who blocked my path and didn't seem to hear me asking him to move. Tripped over a child who appeared out of nowhere.

"Nef, it's me. Wait."

Surely she heard me. She wasn't so far ahead that she didn't. But she never even so much as turned her head. It was only once she had made it all the way across the market and started down a nearby street that I caught up to her.

I grabbed her arm.

"Nef."

She started and dropped her basket.

It was only then I saw her face.

"Sorry." I released her arm and backed away. "Sorry, I thought you were someone else."

The girl crouched, picking up the contents of her basket with trembling hands.

"Let me help you," I said.

"No, I can do it."

"I didn't mean to scare you."

"Please leave me alone."

I backed away. I must have given her an awful fright when I grabbed her like that. The girl packed up her basket, dropping items in with no care as to whether they broke or bruised, then hurried away.

I turned back to the market. Someone knew something. They couldn't have disappeared without a trace.

But they could have. I might spend a year here and never find the captain who transported them. It might be someone who rarely sailed to Suakin. I might never find their trail.

"Tey?"

I hardly heard her over the commotion of the marketplace, absorbed as I was in my thoughts. It wasn't until she spoke again that I noticed. My heart seemed to stutter.

She stood on the edge of the crowd, a basket in her hand, just like the girl I had followed. She was taller than I remembered and her hair was longer. She raised one hand to cover her mouth.

I was frozen.

"You found us," Nef said.

I flung myself across the gap between us. She dropped her basket as I wrapped my arms around her.

"Dear Aten, I was starting to think I would never find you," I said. "Are you all well? Where are Seti and Hennie?"

"At our house," Nef said. She wiped away a tear. "We live not far from here, down that way." She pointed.

"You live here?"

All this time, I had been so close to them and never even knew.

"You are very skinny and your face is a funny colour," she said. "Have you been ill?"

"Very ill. I have been here in Suakin for weeks, but the woman I was staying with fell ill and there was nobody to look after her children. And then I got sick too."

I was rambling. She didn't need to know all this. It could wait until we found the others.

"Come on then," Nef said. She picked up her empty basket. "I am supposed to be getting some vegetables. Then we can go home."

FORTY-SEVEN

TEY

Nef led me through the market confidently, familiar in her task of fetching the vegetables Hennie had asked for. She chattered as we walked, telling me which stalls had the freshest produce and which were to be avoided. It was only as we left the market that she fell quiet. I had expected her to tell me everything that had happened while we were separated, but although she answered my questions, she seemed reluctant to volunteer any information other than about the market.

"Is something wrong?" I asked at last.

She shot me a sideways glance, then pointed to a fallen tree.

"Maybe we should sit for a while," she said.

Unease crept through me.

"What is it?" I asked. "Just tell me."

Nef sat on the tree trunk and carefully arranged her skirt over her legs.

"You should sit, Tey," she said. "You look like you will fall over if you don't."

In truth, I was feeling rather weary, although I wouldn't have admitted it. I sat beside her.

"Go on," I said. "Tell me whatever it is."

She frowned.

"You look terrible," she said. "Our house is not very far away, but you need to rest."

"I am much better than I was."

"Still, it does not hurt to sit for a while. There is no hurry."

"I will sit here and rest if you tell me what has happened since I left you at Tuthmose's house."

"We left the same day you did," she said. "Tuthmose was on his way to his ship. Remember how he was supposed to be leaving for work that day? He never even got out of the village because there were soldiers everywhere. Several squads. He came straight back to warn us. We only had time to grab a few things and then we left."

"I must have just missed them."

Or I left in the opposite direction to their arrival. Would I have seen them had I looked back?

"He showed us how to get away from the village without being seen. It was a very long walk because we had to circle right around. I was so scared. We didn't know if they had guards watching for us to escape, so we could only go a little way at a time, and then we had to hide while Tuthmose checked it was safe to keep going. We didn't have much food and we were all very hungry by the time we got to the harbour. I think it took us three days to get there."

"Tuthmose stayed with you the whole time?"

"Of course he did. He got us onto a ship and we sailed all the way across the Red Sea. But, of course, you know that because you found us."

"Was it Tuthmose who left the message on the windowsill?" I asked.

"He did that while we were packing. He didn't take anything from his own home because he was too busy leaving a message so you could find us. When he told us what he did, I wasn't sure you would figure it out, but Seti said you would."

"She did?"

Nef nodded.

"She knew you would find us. I was not sure." Her cheeks burned. "I am sorry, Tey. I should have known you would."

I patted her hand which lay between us on the trunk. My thoughts whirled.

"How did Tuthmose know there was a ship leaving for Suakin? He must have known before you left."

"I think he heard about it when he went to find work. We had to hide for another couple of days before it sailed. We could have gotten on a different ship earlier, but he said we had to wait for the one to Suakin since that was where the message for you said we would go."

"I would not have found you otherwise," I said. "It was good of him to look after you until you got here."

"He built an extra chamber onto our house, so Seti and I could have our own bedchamber. Grandmother said it was an awful lot of work for two girls, but he knew that was what we wanted. It was very nice of him."

She flushed again.

"He must have lost the work he had arranged," I said. "I hope he didn't have too much trouble securing more work after he brought you here."

"He has not left yet," she said. "He said he would stay until you found us."

"He lives with you?"

I couldn't comprehend why he would have stayed. How long would he have waited if I never found them?

"Of course." She gave me a puzzled look. "Where else would he live? We don't know anyone else here and neither does he."

"Does he know who you are?"

She looked down at her hands and didn't answer.

"Nef?"

"I am sorry, Tey. We knew you wouldn't like it, but he has been really good to us. Grandmother said he deserved to know the truth. We didn't tell him your real name, though. He knows

Tentamun is a cover name, but Grandmother said it was up to you whether you told him."

"But he knows your names? He knows who you really are?"

"We told him everything. And he still stayed and looked after us."

I kept my mouth firmly shut while I digested this.

"Are you awfully mad?" she asked when I didn't reply.

I tried to sort through my feelings before I answered.

"I don't know." It was, at least, an honest answer. "I suppose I am not surprised, but I wish you hadn't told him. The more people who know, the more danger you are in."

"We seem to be in danger anyway." Her tone was bitter in a way I hadn't heard from Nef before. "They keep finding us no matter where we go."

"Maybe we will be safe here. We are a long way from Egypt now."

Was there any limit the chief advisors would stop at to find the girls? They had an entire country at their disposal, especially if it was true that Pharaoh was now the girls' younger brother. I couldn't imagine he would want his sisters hunted like this, but surely a boy of his age — What was he? Eight? Nine? — couldn't stand up to the men who had been his father's most trusted advisors.

But Oracle knew I would come to Suakin. Was this a safe place for us, or was it only that she knew I would find them there? I had so many questions, but she was all the way across the Red Sea and I couldn't ask them.

"Come on," I said, getting to my feet. "Why don't you take me home now?"

∽

The journey continues in Book 3: *Warrior*

The Catalyst has woken and danger is closer than ever before.

KYLIE QUILLINAN

KEEPER
OF THE
BAD THING

A SHORT STORY IN THE WORLD OF
THE AMARNA AGE

ALSO BY KYLIE QUILLINAN

The Amarna Princesses Series

Book One: *Outcast*

Book Two: *Catalyst*

Book Three: *Warrior*

The Amarna Age Series

Book One: *Queen of Egypt*

Book Two: *Son of the Hittites*

Book Three: *Eye of Horus*

Book Four: *Gates of Anubis*

Book Five: *Lady of the Two Lands*

Book Six: *Guardian of the Underworld*

Daughter of the Sun: An Amarna Age Novella

Palace of the Ornaments Series

Book One: *Princess of Babylon*

Book Two: *Ornament of Pharaoh*

Book Three: *Child of the Alliance*

Book Four: *A Game of Senet*

Book Five: *Secrets of Pharaoh*

Book Six: *Hawk of the West*

See kyliequillinan.com for more books, including exclusive collections, and newsletter sign up.

ABOUT THE AUTHOR

Kylie writes about women who defy society's expectations. Her novels are for readers who like fantasy with a basis in history or mythology. Her interests include Dr Who, jellyfish and cocktails. She needs to get fit before the zombies come.

Swan – the epilogue to the Tales of Silver Downs series – is available exclusively to her newsletter subscribers. Sign up at kyliequillinan.com.

Printed in Great Britain
by Amazon

28530558R00130